Published by The Greatest Media

Cover design by The Greatest Media

First Edition
Printed in the United States of America

Special thanks to everyone who
helped make this book possible.
Dolly B,
My baby sister Shaté,
Paulie Knuckles,
My cousin Latoya,
De Fani, Irv, Lady Ty and
everybody chasing
The American Dream.

CHAPTER 1

"Biiiiiitch! You need some money?!" Maddox practically screamed through the phone. I couldn't help but smile. Her energy stayed on ten, always.

"What now, Maddox?" I exhaled, already bracing myself.
"I swear this time it's good money! Easy money. And you need a vacation."

"Wait—what? Where are you?" I asked, but my mind drifted before she could answer. DJ gigs had slowed to a crawl, and I couldn't survive another day under my mother's roof listening to how my twin brother, Amari, was apparently the golden child while I was... whatever she thought I was.

"Vegas, huh?" I said, and she could hear instantly that she had me on the hook.

I opened my mouth to ask the next question, but Maddox—psychic as ever—jumped in. "All-expense-paid trip. Tell me when you can leave and I'll book the ticket right now."

A nervous rush washed over me, the kind you get when you slide all your chips onto one hand at the casino.

To understand why I hesitated, you'd have to rewind—about five hundred and twenty Mondays ago. Back to when I met the Maddox Goldstein of Crown Heights, eons ago when she started dating my twin brother, Amari.

We grew up in Park Slope, but my mother sent us to the same boarding school Maddox's parents shipped her off to upstate NY.

Neither set of parents loved the idea of the Black-Latino boy dating the unusual blonde-haired, dark-blue-eyed Jewish girl. Her parents knew she was brilliant and expected nothing less than greatness in whatever field she touched. Their mistake was believing boarding school would keep her away from the "mean city" they were raising her in.But that was every parent's mistake. They all thought distance would shelter their kids from this cold world. Meanwhile every student walked onto that campus carrying a full suitcase of home, built in habits, trauma, secrets, and all.

That brings us back to Maddox. The spunky little firecracker with swag for days, an attitude that could cut glass, almond-shaped eyes, and a Colgate smile that made people stupid. Captain of the cheer squad, on the chess team, on the swim team, and somehow still the school newspaper editor. But her real love? Hip-hop. And that tiny detail right there turned her whole love life into a perfect storm.

Black boys adored Maddox, and Maddox adored them right back. The jocks would literally form a line at her locker just for the privilege of carrying her books to class. My brother Amari was her first boyfriend back in eighth grade, and once they started dating, that was it. I ended up closer to Maddox than he ever was to her.

We hung out every single day. By the time we left boarding school, we weren't friends anymore, we were family. Now look, I hated her for one whole summer when she broke Amari's heart and cheated on him with some basketball player in 9th grade. But even after they ended things, she and I stayed glued together.

Maddox and I applied to the same colleges, but I ended up back home doing community college so I could stay close to my mother. Maddox headed off to Monroe College in New Rochelle. And of course, my perfect brother floated off to med school at Yale like the golden child he was born to be.

Over those next few years, Maddox changed—matured, leveled up, got sharper. She fell in with this crew at school who were computer hackers. Smart, weird, brilliant kids. She started dating their ringleader, Hasim. A cool Indian kid from California with way too much confidence and, apparently, the knowledge to back it up. He taught her everything: coding, encryption, things that sounded like Mandarin to me.

Before long she switched her major and dove headfirst into the hacker world —what she learned in class during the day, she tested out on the Silk Road at night. By the time she graduated, she'd blown so far past her parents' expectations they didn't even recognize her anymore.
When she moved to San Francisco, she fed them a whole story about landing some big-time tech job. But I knew better.
My girl wasn't interning anywhere. She was running with a crew of what I can only call high-end scammers. Not the petty stuff—this was elite-level, highly organized, million-dollar cybercrime. The kind of syndicates you only hear about on the news.

And right in the middle of it all—like it was nothing—was my cute, chaotic, brilliant friend.

"Hello?!" Maddox snapped, impatience dripping through the phone. "When can I book your flight?"

Truth was, I had absolutely nothing going on. My mother didn't respect my DJ'ing, said it like it was a hobby, not a job. So the idea of escaping that house felt like fresh oxygen.

"Today," I replied, my voice slipping into a low, almost villainous growl.

"Okay, girl!" Maddox squealed, trying and failing to hide her excitement. "I'll text you the itinerary in twenty minutes. Do you have a ride to the airport?
And which one are you leaving from?"

"Yeah, I got one. JFK. How many outfits should I bring?"
"Bring whatever, we'll shop when you get here."

Most people would love to hear that. But I knew better. When Maddox said we'll shop when you get here, it usually meant we'd be running toward something exciting... or away from something dangerous.
Either way—it smelled like trouble.

And honestly? The only reason I went at all... was so I'd have a story to tell you today.

CHAPTER 2

Las Vegas.
I said it to myself quietly as I tore through my dresser drawers and yanked clothes out of my tiny closet. What should I even bring to Vegas? I stood in the middle of my small bedroom, eyes darting around the room like the answer might be hiding in a corner somewhere.

I paid some of the bills here. My mother was on a fixed income, she couldn't manage this place alone, but she still treated me like a disappointment because Amari was in med school and I was a club DJ. Even when I went on tour or flew overseas, she'd still look down her nose at it.

"Mija, why don't you find a nice boy and get married? I'm getting older. I want grandchildren."

Or her other hit single:

"You should stop going out to these clubs at night. No respectable man wants a woman around drunk men and easy women."
She played those tracks weekly.

I needed time away. Badly.

I grabbed every designer thing I owned. The three-year-old Gucci sneakers I bought on sale at the outlet in Jersey, my Louis Vuitton purse that some rich white guy got me when we dated for a few months and every name-brand shirt I could find. Then my phone dinged.

United Flight U683 — JFK — 6:30 AM.What the hell had I gotten myself into?

"A'MAYA! VEN AQUÍ!" my mother yelled from the living room.

That was the exact moment I decided there was no turning back. A small, stubborn part of me prayed this trip would change my life—finally give me the chance to move out of here.

"Yes, Mother?" I sighed as I stepped into the living room.

"Mija, why the attitude?" She waved her hand like she was swatting away a fly. "Anyway, can you get me a glass of ice water from the kitchen?"

She barely looked at me before turning her attention back to Maury blasting from her fifty-inch TV.

I handed her the glass, swallowing the urge to throw it in her face. How lazy can you be? I thought, but kept the words tucked behind my teeth.
"Sit down, sit down. You gotta see this," she said, patting the couch.

"The mother is sleeping with the daughter's husband and she pregnant!" She cackled between breaths, choking on her own laughter.
I love this woman. I hate this woman. Usually at the same time.

But I sat beside her anyway, knowing I didn't know how long I'd be gone. We spent the afternoon watching Maury and Jerry Springer, laughing at people whose lives were somehow messier than ours. This was her comfort show. Chaos and dysfunction served daily.

And for a moment, in between all the noise, I felt the familiar sting of leaving home... and the thrill of finally escaping it.

I didn't tell my mother anything until I was halfway out the door the next morning, catching her while she was half-asleep making her coffee—my best bet to avoid the interrogation I knew she had locked and loaded. I had my bag on my shoulder when she turned around in her robe and matching pink bonnet.

"Where are you going this early?" she croaked in that morning rasp.

"Mom, Maddox got me a gig in Vegas—"

I didn't even get the sentence out before she exploded.

"Oh my God, not Maddox. That girl is trouble. You're gonna give me a heart attack. Don't call me if you go to jail. Diabla. Why must you do these things?"

She would go on forever if I let her. I stepped in, hugged her mid-rant, kissed her cheek, and whispered, "Mom, I'll be fine."

And quietly, in the back of my mind—I prayed that was true.

CHAPTER 3

At the airport, I walked up to the United counter and tried to check in. "I'm sorry, ma'am," the agent said, tapping her screen. "Your ticket has been canceled."

I should've taken that as the first red flag.

I texted Maddox immediately. No response. I called. Straight to voicemail. A few minutes later, she texted back: Give me a few minutes.
A "few minutes" turned into an hour. Then another. My patience was chewing through its leash. Just when I was about to go home, she finally texted:
DELTA FLIGHT 1438. LEAVES IN 15 MINUTES.

I grabbed my bags and hauled ass across the airport like my life depended on it. I didn't even notice the ticket said first class until I was boarding.

The second I sat down, I fell in love.

I usually sit in the back, damn near on the jump seat with the flight attendants. But these seats? Lush. Roomy. A little piece of heaven in the sky. On that five-hour flight, I said yes to everything they offered. Drinks, snacks, more drinks.

By the time we landed, I was drunk and had made a new friend: Brian from Miami now living in West Hollywood. Geeky, funny, talkative, definitely not my type, but entertaining enough to keep the flight interesting. He kept flirting a little, but harmlessly.

We talked about why we were both headed to LA. I told him I was visiting my childhood best friend. He told me he was originally from Florida but had moved to LA alone for a good job.

Cute little Brian from West Hollywood.

He had no idea he'd end up saving my life later.

I texted Maddox the second I landed, and she hit me right back:

There's a car outside waiting.

Brian and I grabbed our luggage and walked out still laughing at the dumb jokes we traded on the plane. A black Cadillac truck slid up to the curb, windows tinted, engine humming like money. The driver rolled down the window and asked if I was Amaya in a thick Middle Eastern accent.

"Some friends you've got," Brian joked.

We exchanged numbers, and he helped the driver load my bag before I climbed in. The moment the doors shut and we pulled off, something in me cracked open. The palm trees waved like they recognized me. The warm air wrapped around me like a welcome-back hug. Every turn we made, the city lights winked at me like they knew a secret.

I had no idea where I was going until we swung into the valet at the Wynn Encore.

As soon as I stepped out, my phone buzzed.

32nd floor. Maddox, right on time.

Walking through that hotel felt like stepping into another world. Everything glowed. Everything sparkled. The décor looked like Alice in Wonderland had money. Huge, bold flowers wrapped in white lights, floors so colorful they almost moved under my feet. I kept slowing down just trying to take it all in. Even the elevators were an experience, all glass with a view of the Strip stretching out forever.

I should've noticed that red flag too—nothing about this was normal.

Maddox, what the hell are you into now?

When the elevator finally dinged on the 32nd floor, the doors opened to a woman I barely recognized. Gone was the messy-bun Maddox who used to steal my lip gloss. This Maddox was grown, and shaped more like my family than hers.

Money looked good on her. Her blue eyes had a sharpness to them now, a heat. And that same smile she used to get her way as a kid? It had a whole Dr. Jekyll twist to it.

She looked like luxury head-to-toe, and suddenly I felt dumb for packing my little "designer-if-you-squint" outfits from home.

"A'MAYA!" she screamed, throwing her arms around me.

She hugged me so hard I lost my breath.

"I missed you too, Maddie the Baddie," I said and I meant it.

My wild, reckless friend who disappeared into the West Coast right after college and never looked back... yeah, I missed her.

We swayed there for a few seconds, just holding on, before she grabbed my hand and yanked me down the hallway.

"You have to meet Biggs and Sabrina the Creamer," she said, speed-walking like she was late to her own heist.

"Sabrina the who?" I muttered, already bracing myself for whatever madness was waiting behind that door.

Once we stepped inside the room, I tried to play it cool, but the view was ridiculous. Floor-to-ceiling glass wrapping around a corner suite like we just walked into Heaven's VIP section.

"This is my best friend A'Maya I keep telling y'all about," Maddox announces, guiding me toward a man shaped like a luxury snowman. Big on top, skinny legs holding up the whole operation.

"A'Maya, this is Biggs. My partner."

Biggs had to be 6'5, maybe 6'6. A shiny bald head but a sharp taper around the sides. His eyes pushed forward like he sucked on a lemon, his outfit screamed money, and his cologne hit me before he got within ten feet of each other. But when he grinned...the chapped lips and crowded teeth told a completely different story. His watch lit up the whole room like a disco ball as he reached out.

"Nice to meet you, shawty," he says in a southern accent I couldn't place yet.
"And this is Sabrina. Adult movie star," he adds, looking at her like she's his prized student.

Sabrina steps forward from the bed area. Tiny thing, maybe 5'1, soft low voice, dressed way more regular than what I expected from somebody whose job title ends with "star." She had black, long silky hair that draped around her perfectly chiseled face. Sabrina's dark green eyes almost made you feel like she could see through you.
Still unsure what the hell I just walked into, I shoot a look at Maddox and blurt out,
"I'm not fucking on camera."
The whole room explodes in laughter like I just told the best joke of the year.

"Go freshen up. We're going to dinner," Maddox says, still giggling. "I'll explain everything. And don't worry...no one's making you have sex with anybody. Unless you want to." She cracks up again as Biggs and Sabrina join in on the joke.

Still confused as hell, I head into the large luxurious bathroom to change.
I threw something together quick, but I'm me. I look good in anything. My parents passed down style like a family heirloom.
When I came out, somehow everyone had changed clothes too. Now they all matched. Black, crispy, clean, and professional. Biggs gave me this tight-lipped smile, wide as his shoulders.

"Let's go," Maddox says, already heading to the door.
In the elevator, four different expensive colognes battled for dominance. You could tell all of us basically showered in our scents before leaving.

I was anxious, sure, but the thrill sat right on top of it. Biggs wasn't handsome, but he had that kind of command-your-attention confidence. The type that fills a room before he even walks into it.
Sabrina looked like a caramel-complexioned barbie doll. She kept a innocent aura but every now and then this flash of danger slipped through like lightning behind clouds. Maddox, on the other hand, wore a black one-piece dress that clung in all the right places and floated behind her like it knew who it belonged to. She walked like a woman who could stop traffic without turning her head.

And then there was me.

We didn't plan it, but somehow I ended up in all black too. My hair was long, shiny, blown straight and swinging down my back like it had choreography. A black spandex outfit hugged my body, paired with a short rock and roll leather jacket and Rick Owens boots that completed the look. I caught a glimpse of us in a mirrored column on the way in, three beautiful women flanking Biggs. I wondered if he felt like the king of the universe guiding us into Capital Grille.

Once we sat down, reality smacked me. How much money did I even bring? Could I afford water? I quietly settled on ordering soup. Maddox leaned in like she could hear my thoughts and whispered,

"Order what you want. We got it." Then winked.

It was comforting... and unsettling.

People don't pay for you like that unless they want something back.

"Let's get a round of shots! Waiter! Four doubles of Patrón!" Biggs boomed across the restaurant, his voice slicing right through the room.

Doubles? My spirit left my body for a second.

But once that liquid heat hit our systems, the whole vibe loosened up. They ordered a seafood tower the size of a wedding cake, appetizers, and more drinks. Meanwhile my mind kept replaying the same question on a loop:

What the hell is going on?

The restaurant manager even came over with a complimentary bottle of champagne. Biggs's personality was so big he practically owned the whole place. Already talking to couples at nearby tables like he knew them his whole life.

Maddox caught my eye, tilted her head toward the exit. I followed her out, noticing Sabrina out the corner of my eye. She was smiling, but barely. She looked like she was board. A woman who is used to all the attention doesn't want to see her man entertaining anyone else.

Outside, Maddox shocked the life out of me by lighting a cigarette.

"Hey A'maya," she said, inhaling deep like she was in a perfume ad.
"Hey Maddox. And seriously, thank you. But girl... what do y'all want me to do? I'm not into high-class escorting, or whatever this is. No shade, but I—"

"A'Maya... breathe." She laughed mid-exhale while I realized I was spiraling.

"It's nothing like that. We're here in Vegas for a few days, then L.A. I'll tell you everything then. If you like it, stay. If not, you go home with new clothes and good memories. Simple."

She took another drag like we were discussing brunch plans.
"I just want you to meet my team. See what we do."

Maddox always had a way of talking people into things, and here I was—held hostage by my own curiosity.
"Okay... but this better not be anything wild."
"It's not," she said, dropping the cigarette, stamping it out. Her smile curled into something... mischievous.

Not evil, but not angelic either.
When we walked back in, someone new was at the table—and he stood up when he saw us. My breath snagged.

A tall, dark golden brown Filipino (at least that's what I guessed) lean, muscular, covered in tattoos that told their own stories. Buzzed sides, long silky hair tied in a clean ponytail. Thin mustache, sharp chin beard. His face had this quiet pain, and his eyes held a whole history of disappointment and survival.

"Ice, this is my best friend A'maya," Maddox said.

He didn't look away from me as he spoke.

"Well, nice to meet you, Miss A'maya," he said, voice deep and smooth with the same accent Biggs carried.

I felt myself blush and turned away before I melted right there.

"Hi... Ice," I managed.

"Aye, y'all, we're wrapping up here. Gonna head over and see the rest of the family," Biggs announced, already on his feet.

Walking out, I nudged Maddox. "Where's Ice's girl?"

Maddox didn't blink. "He's a whole pimp, A'maya."

"Oh... he's a player," I said, already disappointed.

"No, babe. A pimp. Girls bring him money. He has a stable. A real pimp."

I didn't know which crushed me more—him being fine as hell... or him being fine as hell with a roster of women he profits from.

Outside, a line of black trucks waited for us like we were some VIP entourage. We split up into different ones and headed to TAO. Inside, a table of about twenty people stood as soon as Biggs walked in. The respect was instant. We followed behind him like honored guests, smiling and nodding at strangers who greeted us like cousins at a reunion.

The music thundered through the room, too loud for names or formal introductions.

Once we sat, I finally took everyone in—faces, bodies, energy. Every woman at that table, every single one, was gorgeous. A few had flawless BBLs, snatched waists, glossy hair. Others were naturally built or athletic, skin glowing like they were dipped in gold shimmer. Diamonds, fresh nails, soft hands, designer bags.
My head started spinning.
Is everyone here a sex worker?
And more importantly—
What did I just sign myself up for?

Biggs sat at the head of the table, and that alone told me everything I needed to know. The men around him looked like the cast of some underground mob flick—except more diverse, more dangerous, and definitely more expensive.

Most were Black, muscular, bearded—big wrists wrapped in diamond-encrusted watches, shirts tight across their chests, smelling like cologne you only find behind glass. A few were Asian, built like they trained in violence, tattoos crawling from their sleeves up their necks.
Each carried scars like souvenirs from lives they probably never talk about. Even the two white guys looked like Hollywood trouble—Brad Pitt jawlines, Tom Cruise confidence, covered in ink, eyes full of pain they'd never admit.

It was a strange, beautiful, intimidating circus.

And I was drunk.

Which did not help the panic brewing in my chest.

I had to get it together.

Maddox is right. Enjoy the next few days. You deserve it, A'maya.

I repeated it like a mantra until my pulse slowed.

Back at the hotel, Maddox and I split from Biggs and Sabrina at the elevators and headed to our own room. The second I saw twin beds, I could've cried tears of relief. I didn't care if they were hard as marble.

Maddox was as smashed as I was. She collapsed onto her bed in full glam: heels, dress, lashes, everything. Legs half hanging off like a mannequin someone forgot to pose. Within seconds she was knocked out, lightly snoring like a cute drunk auntie.

I remembered I left my bag in Biggs' room, so I wandered down the quiet hallway and knocked. It took a minute, but Sabrina eventually cracked the door, blushing in a plush hotel robe.

"Hey A'maya," she whispered, cheeks pink.

"Hey, Sabrina... can I grab my bag real quick?"

"One sec," she said, shutting the door fast.

When she returned, she handed me my bag with both hands like it was fragile.

"Big Daddy isn't dressed for company right now. I hope you understand."

She smiled sweetly, then closed the door before I could figure out how to feel about that.

Too tipsy to process the whole situation, I drifted back to my room. Maddox's quiet little drunk snore bounced off the walls while I got ready for bed. I had to give Sabrina credit—she repacked my bag neater than I ever could've.

I'd eventually learn the reason behind her precision.

The last thing I saw before my eyes shut was the view—Vegas sky fading from purple to pink, the sun climbing behind distant mountains like it was sneaking up on the world.

"Goooood morning, Maya baby!"

Maddox's voice hit me like a glass bottle shattering.

I sat up so fast my neck popped.

"What time is it?" I croaked.

8:46 a.m.

I hadn't even slept a full two hours. Champagne fumes were still dancing in my throat.

"Time to go, beautiful! The guys are meeting us downstairs. We're grabbing breakfast. Pack your bag—we can shower at the next hotel. You got five minutes. Chop chop!"

I sat there blinking, trying to figure out if this was real or if I was trapped in some chaotic dream sequence. Maddox tore through the room like it was on fire before spinning back around:

"Let's go, A'maya!"

Thankfully my things were still packed. I shoved my feet into my boots, threw on Dior sunglasses big enough to hide my whole morning-face situation, and followed her to the elevator.

My breath was kicking like a martial arts movie, but I wasn't about to ask questions yet. I needed water. And silence. And maybe a new liver.

Outside, Biggs, Sabrina, and Ice were already waiting inside a black Escalade. The driver loaded our bags, and I basically melted into the backseat. My head touched the window for maybe sixty seconds before Maddox tapped my arm.

Everyone was already outside.

How do they keep teleporting?!

I slid out of the truck half-asleep and saw the sign: Hash House.

At least we were getting food.

The order sounded like we were feeding a football team: pancakes the size of steering wheels, chicken and waffles that needed their own zip code, omelets, scrambles, sides, fruit... Maddox ordered five things like always, nibbling a few bites of each. Biggs ordered three full meals and cleaned all of them.
Sabrina and Ice ordered the healthiest things on the menu like they were prepping for a photoshoot.
And of course—alcohol.
Mimosas, shots, sangria, Baileys in the coffee.
It didn't matter the hour—something had to burn going down.
Ice didn't drink, though. His escape was weed.

He invited me outside while we waited. And out there, he was... different. Calm. Charming. Articulate. Not the stereotypical pimp caricature people imagine. I could see exactly why girls fell for him—too bad I already mentally categorized him as "the bro."

"So, where you from, shawty?" he asked, flashing a full grill of gold teeth.
"Brooklyn," I said, with the thickest New York accent I've ever used in my life.
"Naaah, what part? I got folks out that way."

He stepped closer, smiling like we had all the time in the world...
and the story was just getting started.

He talked while rolling the joint, hands moving so fast I had to blink twice just to keep up. In less than thirty seconds he twisted that thing to perfection—tight, smooth, clean edges like a professional. Honestly? It deserved a Guinness World Record. Or a spot on one of those game shows where people do impossible stunts with deadly calm. Every time he finished a sentence, he flashed that small mischievous grin—like his mouth knew secrets his words didn't bother explaining.

"Park Slope. What you know about Brooklyn?" I asked, side-eyeing him.

"My cousin on Empire Blvd," he said, with a drawl that didn't belong to any coast I could name. As he spoke, he lifted his hand to wave at a car with blacked-out windows rolling through the lot.

The car stopped right in front of us.

And out hopped the coolest Mexican man I've ever seen.

He had the same vibe as Ice—like they were cousins in spirit if not blood. They hugged like brothers who'd survived something together.

"Malik, this A'maya. Maddox peoples from back East," Ice said, passing him the joint.

"What's good, lil sis," Malik exhaled, voice dipped in that West Coast Hispanic accent I swear only exists in movies.

"What's good, Malik."

The name threw me. He had the blackest name I've ever heard on a latino, yet he was one of the most effortlessly cool men I'd ever met.

Malik handed Ice a brown paper bag. Ice peeked inside and pulled out the biggest bag of weed I've ever seen in my life. No exaggeration—this looked like a wholesale order.

They kept passing the joint back and forth before offering it to me.

Why not?

I was on vacation.

The first inhale tasted fresh and smoky, clean in a way that surprised me. It hit my head instantly. I took one more pull to avoid looking lame—and that was the mistake that sent me straight to outer space. The joint was the width of a grown man's finger. By the time I passed it back, my knees were threatening to quit on me entirely.

Ice tossed the bag in his backpack, they exchanged quick goodbyes, and we headed back inside.

I sat down at the table feeling like I'd just crash-landed from Mars. Maddox looked at me and burst out laughing.

"Girl, are you okay?"

I turned, smiled, nodded—

but the words never made it out of my mouth.

Ice answered for me.

"Nah, she high as giraffe nuts."

The whole table cracked up as I tried to blink myself back to Earth. I reached for a little bit of everything on the table like everyone else was doing. No way was I touching more alcohol—mixing that with this high would've taken me out for the entire week.

I ordered a double espresso and prayed I'd descend from the moon sometime before noon.

Then the check arrived.

Biggs slid a card to the waiter without hesitation.

A moment later the waiter returned, clearing his throat.

"Sir, this card was declined. Do you have another form of payment?"

The smiles around the table evaporated. Expressions shifted—nervous, guilty, embarrassed.

Biggs laughed it off and handed over another card.

A beat passed.

The waiter came back again.

"Sir, this one is declined as well."

Ice cut in before the awkwardness could stretch any further.

"Hey man, how much is it?"

"$568.42," Biggs said, glancing at the receipt. "Must've left the new cards at the house."

Ice didn't blink. He pulled out a thick wad of cash—clean bills—and counted out, "Six hundred, six-twenty. Keep the change."
He passed the money down the table like it was nothing.

Now I was really confused.
Why was Ice paying?

Why did we leave the hotel so damn early?
Why did everyone look so tense?

Maddox looked at her phone and said, "The car is outside," without looking at any of us.

Outside, our bags were still in the trunk. Same driver, same Escalade. Biggs and Maddox were having some intense whisper-argument beside the truck while Ice watched from inside like he never blinked.

Then Maddox dug into her bag and handed Biggs what looked like a stack of credit cards. They started calling the numbers on the back of each one, checking balances. Every time Maddox didn't like what she heard, she dropped the card onto the asphalt like it had betrayed her. Soon they had two piles: the "maybe" stack in their hand, and the "hell no" stack scattered on the ground.
"Pick them up," Biggs snapped. "Can't be leaving shit out here like this."

When they got back in, Maddox kept her head down, scrolling or texting. Biggs exhaled heavily and told the driver:
"Fontainebleau."

We walked into the lobby and I almost forgot my own name.
Everything was white, glowing, futuristic—like a luxury spaceship for rich people who'd finally colonized Mars. I had to silently remind myself: Act like you been somewhere, girl.

Biggs checked us in and booked three panorama suites on the same floor. As soon as we split up, I dragged myself to my room praying for two things:
A blistering hot shower,

and sleep so deep I forgot my own story.
We stepped out of Gucci with our bags like we had just robbed the place in broad daylight. The second our feet hit the marble floor I could feel Maddox's energy shift, her shoulders relaxed, her breath released, and she slipped her sunglasses down her nose like she'd just finished a heist and lived to tell about it. Sabrina was right beside her, fixing her hair like someone who had trained for moments exactly like this.

I didn't know the next move, so I stayed glued to them like a magnet. The center of Crystals looked like a luxury aquarium. Glass walls, neon reflections, people gliding by in designer everything. And there we were, shopping bags dangling from our elbows like everything was normal. Like nothing about what just happened was insane.
We cut through the crowd and ran into the rest of the group at the escalators. They appeared at the same time like they got a group notification—Voltron, assemble. Biggs was carrying bags too—Louis Vuitton, Dior, two from Bottega—his face unreadable except for that slight grin he always had, the one that told me he was enjoying whatever chaos he'd created today.

Ice saw us and cracked a smile. "There go the Gucci girls," he teased, reaching for one of Sabrina's bags to take the weight off her. Sweet in a big-brother way, but with that street-slick awareness like he was watching everything at once. Malik wasn't with him, but his presence still lingered. Loud energy even in silence.

We walked like a pack of wolves, all moving fast without looking like we were in a hurry. No talking, just the rhythm of security guards eyeing us from a distance and tourists pretending not to stare. Luxury stores reflect your face whether you want them to or not, and I caught myself in the mirrored walls—eyes wide, mouth slightly open, walking in a world I knew damn well wasn't mine.

CHAPTER 4

We hit the exit where the desert heat slapped me like I owed it money. The black truck rolled up almost instantly, like it had been circling the block waiting for us to reappear. Same driver, same expressionless face, like he'd seen this all before. Once we piled in, the tension thickened again. No one talked. The ride felt longer than it should've been. You know those car rides where everyone's staring out the window pretending the world looks interesting? That was us. Except Biggs kept rubbing his temples and Maddox kept checking over her shoulder like she expected someone to follow.

I sat in the middle row next to Sabrina, who kept whispering affirmations under her breath like she was trying to manifest good credit.

Finally, Ice broke the silence.

"So... where we headed now? Another store?" he said with half a laugh.

"Nah," Biggs snapped a little too sharply. "We done."

Maddox shot him a look. One of those silent conversations couples have that says way more than words. Something was off. More off than before. And I wasn't sure if I should be scared or just buckle up.

The truck pulled up to the Fontainebleau again, and the driver hopped out to open the doors. As soon as the bags were out of the trunk, Maddox motioned for me to stay close.

"Don't wander," she murmured. That alone made my stomach clench.

We walked through the lobby, all those marble floors and white walls glowing like heaven's waiting room. The kind of place where money breathes differently.

Everybody walking around in linen and diamonds.

Meanwhile, my anxiety was tap dancing in my chest.

Biggs handled check-ins like he owned the whole chain, dropping cards and IDs on the counter with confidence that didn't match the two declined cards from earlier.

He secured three panorama rooms on the same floor—three of them. Like it was nothing.

We finally got upstairs. Everyone split off in different directions, mumbling about needing showers or naps or "handling business."

The second I got into my room, I shut the door behind me and leaned against it. My heart pounding, mind spinning, bags slipping from my fingers onto the carpet.

I wanted answers. I wanted clarity. I wanted sleep.

But Maddox had other plans.

Maddox walked in like the room already belonged to her and made a straight line for the desk. She unloaded that little travel-sized command center she carried everywhere—a slim laptop, some kind of external hard drive, and a small machine that looked way too much like it printed cards for comfort.

I wanted to ask a million questions, but my brain was fried. Between the flight, the weed, the chaos, and zero sleep, my thoughts were walking into each other like drunk people. The view outside was ridiculous—skyline, blue water, everything sparkling—but I didn't even have it in me to look twice.

Before I could pull my shirt off, Maddox stood up with her phone already pointed at me.

"Put your back against the wall real quick," she said.

"Huh? I look crazy," I protested, trying to shield my face.

"You look fine." She was already walking toward me, face serious like she was taking passport photos at TSA.

"What's this for?" I asked, flattening myself against the wall.

"For traveling with us. We keep pictures of everyone that rolls with us. You'll see."

"Maddox, what the fuck?"

She gave me that calming, dangerous smile. "I promise it'll all make sense, A'maya."

Then the flash popped. And another. I let her take a few before waving her off.

"Okay, that's enough. You better not have me in no shit!"

She scrolled through the photos and laughed. "I'd die before I let anything happen to you."

Then she sat back down, connected her phone to the laptop, and started typing like her fingers were running a marathon. That was my cue to give up on understanding anything tonight. I headed for the shower. Exhausted, confused, and wondering how I even ended up on this trip.

When I came out in a towel, Maddox was knocked out sitting against the wall, head tilted, mouth slightly open, with four freshly printed credit cards fanned out on the carpet beside her like a deck she'd been shuffling. I put on my pajamas and gently woke her.

Her eyes snapped open. The second she realized she fell asleep mid-crime, she jolted upright and dove right back into her work like nothing happened. I stood there staring at her, anxiety tying tight little knots in my stomach.

"Maddox," I said softly.

She didn't even look up. "I promise you're safe and have nothing to worry about."

That reassurance wasn't worth a damn, but I clung to it anyway.

"Get some sleep. We're going out in a few hours," she added, eyes glued to the screen.

Il nodded. What else could I do?

The bed felt like God made it Himself. The pillows swallowed my head, the blankets hugged me, and the mattress felt like being held by a cloud. I melted into it instantly.

Somewhere between life and death, I heard my name in the sweetest tone.
I opened my eyes and there she was, fully dressed like she hadn't slept at all.
Maddox smiled, calm and composed.
"We'll be downstairs."
rolled my eyes. No pressure. Just the whole clique waiting on me to catch up.
Ugh.

I rushed to get ready, but I couldn't compete with Maddox. She had on a Versace button-up, tailored pants, red-bottom Louboutins, her hair in a sleek bun, red lipstick, and oversized sunglasses that looked like something Jackie Onassis would've begged for

.

Me? I grabbed a fitted button-up from Express, dark blue stretch jeans from Gap, and my Gucci sneakers. I beat my face to perfection, slicked my hair into a high ponytail, and prayed it was enough.

Downstairs, they were all dressed like they were going on tour. Coordinated, confident, ready. We had another black truck waiting and headed straight to the Shops at Crystals.

Once inside, it felt like walking onto a movie set. The same people from dinner appeared like they'd been summoned—moving as a unit before splitting off like they had assigned territory. Dior, Louis Vuitton, Bottega, Hermès, Cartier—everywhere I turned, somebody from the group was shopping like money wasn't a real thing.

Maddox, Sabrina, and I ended up in Gucci. Since I didn't know protocol, I hovered and window-shopped like a lost kid.

Then I noticed Maddox and Sabrina pulling pieces off hangers like they had a personal stylist on payroll.

I leaned in close and whispered, "What do I do?"

Without even glancing at me she said,

"Get some clothes, girl. We need to upgrade your look. Get some things for you and some to sell."

To sell?

Okay, I was officially keeping a mental list of questions.

I grabbed a pair of black heels, a dress, a T-shirt, a hat, a belt, and two pairs of sunglasses—half for me, half for... whatever hustle they were running.

At the counter Maddox still had her sunglasses on, body tight like she was bracing for impact. Sabrina pretended to fix her makeup but she kept checking the card reader like it might bite her.

"$11,983.24," the cashier said, straight-faced.

Maddox handed her the card without turning her head. Both she and Sabrina held their breath until we heard the click and the printer start rolling.

The cashier bagged everything up neatly. The second those bags were in our hands, the three of us speed-walked out like we had a getaway car outside.

I didn't know where we were going next but wherever it was,

I stayed right on their heels.

The fear and the rush of adrenaline that ran through me is indescribable. Somehow the rest of the gang had the same results and we all met back up in unison, bags from each luxury department store swinging like trophies as we headed out the front entrance.

Outside, Biggs, Maddox, and I broke off and climbed into our own Escalade with a driver and went straight back toward the hotel.
In the car Maddox leaned forward, talking to Biggs like she was giving a status report.

"It's her first run, so I told her to grab a few things for her closet."
I jumped in quickly, feeling like I needed to defend myself.
"I only got a dress, heels, and a pair of glasses for me. But there's a belt, a hat, glasses and a T-shirt in there. I did what Maddox said!"

The whole car burst into laughter. I felt my face heat but tried to laugh with them.
"Maddox is gonna school you for the next trip,"
Biggs rumbled. His drawl wrapped around the words like honey on gravel. "But job well done, lil sis."
I nodded, but I stayed quiet.
I genuinely didn't know what job I just did.
By the time we reached the valet, Maddox had already switched into her efficient mode. She grabbed our Gucci bags,
sorted out which were mine, and pressed the room key into my hand.
"I'll be back shortly."
Then she dug into her purse and peeled off a wad of twenties—must've been around $360—and handed it to me.

"Go to the bar or order room service."

Before I could respond, she and Biggs were already back in the truck.

The driver shut the trunk. Sabrina was drifting toward the hotel entrance like she had all the time in the world. I practically jogged to catch up.

"What you about to do?" I asked, trying to sound casual.

She turned with the sweetest, softest smile, like honey melting in warm tea.

"Whatever you wanna do, sugar. Wanna go to the bar? Or one of these many restaurants?"

I didn't know anything about this place or what was around it—or honestly, what planet I was on at this point.

"I could use a drink... and maybe a small bite."

"Alright then, let's go to the tavern!" she chirped, looping her arm through mine and guiding me like we'd known each other years.

Sabrina moved with this mix of innocence and charm, topped with that Southern hospitality sweetness. I still couldn't wrap my head around how she was an adult film star until the bartender recognized her the second we sat down.

"Oh my god, I can't believe it's you," he blurted. He was middle-aged, in shape, with a salt-and-pepper haircut and matching goatee.

Sabrina blushed like she wasn't used to it.

"Ladies, please sit. My name is Guy and I'll be serving you tonight."

"In which way, daddy?" she purred, licking her top teeth slow enough to ruin marriages.

Guy froze, cheeks red, like she'd unplugged his brain for a moment.

"I'll have a martini, dirty of course. And she'll have a..."

I panicked internally. I'm not a drinker.

"Um... long island iced tea."

Sabrina stared at me like I had just ordered diesel fuel.

"What are you, a trucker?" she snapped.

"She'll have a lemon drop—with tequila instead of vodka."

She sucked her teeth slowly at him, and Guy pretty much evaporated back behind the bar to make the drinks.

"I make them uncomfortable before they get to do it to me," Sabrina explained, crossing her legs. "If they recognize me, sometimes they get disrespectful, or they're testing me. If I don't say anything sexual, he might be disappointed and kill his lil fantasy. Or I'm testin' him to see how the night's gonna go."

I didn't say a word. I just listened, absorbing every scrap of this world I somehow fell into.

Guy came back with our drinks, shoulders back, courage gathered.
"Drinks on the house, ladies," he said, winking at Sabrina.
"Darlin', these drinks are safe, right? I'm not gonna pass out in here, am I?" she asked, voice sultry but sharp underneath.
Guy immediately wilted.

"I would *never.*"

"No baby, listen..." She leaned forward just slightly, voice trembling just enough to sound poetic. "It's so scary out here in this mean world. I'm all alone and don't have a strong man like you to protect me. You work out, don't you Guy? What's your Instagram?"

She handed him her phone like she was giving him a blessing.
He typed with the enthusiasm of a teenager, barely looking down.
"I know it must be hard for you, beautiful," he said softly. "Everywhere you go not knowing who to trust."

"Thank you for these drinks... and follow back, daddy." She sipped her martini while keeping eye contact. Deadly. Just deadly.
A man down the bar yelled, "Excuse me, can I order a drink?"
Guy snapped out of his trance.

"Enjoy your drinks, ladies," he said, shuffling away.

Sabrina cracked up.

"Girl you can't be too safe out here. Got his IG in case he's a creep. And if I'm ever here again—free drinks. The gift that keeps giving."

Her lemon drop was strong; by sip number three I could feel my edges blurring.

"Sabrina... can I ask you something?"

"Of course, darling."

"How'd you get into adult film?"

"Why? You wanna get into it?" she deadpanned.

"No! Hell no. I mean—not that there's anything wrong with it. I just—"

"It's okay, I'm messin' with you," she said, cutting me off with a laugh. "I know what you mean."

Then her voice softened, and a shadow passed behind her eyes.

"I'm from a poor small farm town in Alabama where nothing happens but the weather changing. I hated it there. My daddy was my mama's uncle.

She never told nobody about that affair. He kept taking advantage of her up until she was 16 years old and got pregnant.

She blamed her boyfriend but I didn't look anything like him when I was born so they knew that was a lie. She never told out of fear. I mean how can you tell your daddy his brother is raping you.

When I turned 11, that same uncle started touching me. A sit on the lap when he was hard, of lifting me up while playing but touching my as.
My mama knew the signs and lost her mind.
She killed him. Shot him dead in front of me one night when she was drunk and saw him fondle me. She's in jail doing 20 to life."

"That night I stayed in a nice hotel. Ate whatever I wanted. After that, I kept getting booked because there wasn't much I'd turn down. The producers loved my look and kept me on payroll " She smiled sadly over the rim of her martini.
I had so many questions but didn't want to cross a line.

"So... how'd you meet Biggs and Ice?"

Guy dropped off our second round, and she took it without breaking eye contact with me.

"I met Biggs a few months ago here in Vegas. I was with another John, and I saw Biggs spending big and winning bigger.
He recognized me and kept following me when I was alone—begging for a date. Movie money is cute, but I need to keep paid between films if you catch my drift." She winked.

" I have expensive taste. When I was done with my other client I texted Biggs. We discussed prices and my stipulations. We had a blast you hear me? I was shocked that chubby man could keep up with me! We made love like hundred times that night. The next morning after he paid me, I asked him what he does. He hesitated—or acted like he did—then told me his operation."

I waited.

She stopped.

"...And what is that?" I finally asked.

She stared at me like she was genuinely confused.

"So you don't know?"

I shook my head no, feeling the alcohol and embarrassment mixing into a warm nausea.

She studied my face for a long moment.

"Honey... you gotta talk to your friend. Let her explain everything. It's not my place."

My stomach twisted because she was right—it was time to stop pretending I wasn't in the middle of something big.

I just smiled. "Heard you."

The vibe shifted after that, and I felt this pressure to keep things light, so I pulled a random question out of the air. "You ever been to New York City?"

Sabrina perked up. "Yes, I have as a matter of fact. I worked... well, you know why I was there." She blushed.

"Did you get to enjoy the city or just work?"

"I saw Times Square, ate at Mr. Chow's. That was exciting.
Oh—and I saw Central Park." We were warming back up when Maddox appeared behind us. I figured Sabrina texted her our location.

Biggs moved straight to the bar and told the bartender to put our drinks on the room. Guy puffed up like he was marking territory. "They're on the house," he declared.

Biggs and Guy had this ten-second alpha stare-off before Biggs chuckled and walked away. Sabrina lived for the moment. She turned, winked at Guy on our way out, and he winked back like he was under a spell.

CHAPTER 5

Back upstairs in the room, Maddox handed me $600. I stared at it like it was counterfeit.

"When we pop," she explained, "whatever we leave with, we get fifty percent of the value. Then y'all get fifty percent of that."

I nodded like I understood. In reality she might as well have been explaining quantum physics. Something about fifty percent of the fifty percent of the fifty percent of the new fifty percent—whatever. Money appeared. That's all I caught.

She wasn't done. "And A'maya... only talk to me about what's going on. Nobody else."

Oh, so Sabrina snitched. Great.

"I want you to ask me anything. But you're my peoples. You talk to me."

"Okay, but you told me I had to wait till we got to L.A., and I don't even know when that is."

"You're right," she admitted. "And that's tonight. So pack your bags. Twenty minutes."

"Wait—what?!"

She just walked out cold, the door slamming like a period to the sentence.

I stood there, fully thinking about disappearing to the airport. I had almost a thousand dollars, a new outfit, and a growing fear I was wrapped up in something way above my comfort level. Brentwood? Wasn't that the O.J. neighborhood? Why the hell were we going there?

Outside the hotel a silver stretch Range Rover was waiting, Ice and Biggs already inside. Biggs lifted a glass of champagne in one hand and the bottle in the other.

"Y'all coming?"

That annoying grin was all trouble. And there I went, hopping right in.

Sabrina was missing but I wasn't asking questions. Ever again. Not after the betrayal Olympics she ran earlier.

We grabbed food from the Crack Shack and hit the almost four hour trip to Cali.

Ice rolled blunt after blunt, hotboxing the entire truck until I was sure the driver was high off secondhand smoke.

"Maddox tells me you a famous DJ," Ice grinned, gold teeth shining like headlights.

"I don't know about famous, but I'm aight."

"What name you go by?" Biggs asked.

"DJ 1 Chance," I said. "Everywhere I went people told me no. I'd tell them I just need one chance. At a DJ battle the host misheard me, kept announcing me as 1 Chance. I won the battle, so it stuck."

Biggs nodded like a proud uncle. "I like that. Here's to 1 Chance."

He lifted his glass. We toasted. We laughed. We ate. We smoked. And eventually, we all knocked out.

I woke up to voices outside the car—Biggs talking to the driver, Maddox by the gate. She punched in a code and the metal doors peeled open like we were entering a billionaire's hideaway.

Inside looked like wealth had a baby with old-money tradition. Split-wall railings, expensive art everywhere, signed footballs in glass cases, jerseys from every league. Whoever lived here didn't just have money—they had history.

I picked a bedroom and started unpacking before Maddox walked in and shut the door behind her.

"Hey A'maya," she started, calm. "First things first—we never fully unpack. Makes it easier to leave when we need to."

I snapped. "Okay, look... this feels like murderers are chasing us. Like we're on the run from the law."

"You're not that far off."

"What?!"

She sighed. "Let me tell you everything since I left Brooklyn. Can we smoke by the pool?"

I just nodded.

As we walked through the hallway, Ice strutted by with some girl our age. Pale, ice-blue eyes, long blonde hair, and the coldest aura.

"This is Malinda," Ice introduced. She didn't smile—just looked.

Maddox gave a tiny nod and kept walking. I offered a quick wave and hurried behind her.

Outside, the pool shimmered under the moonlight. We dropped into these plush lawn chairs, way more comfortable than anything I owned, and lit up.

Maddox inhaled slow, her eyes on the water.

"Okay, A'maya. After I left New York with Hasim, we moved to San Jose. He built an operation—a whole little family. Everyone had a role. Mine was finding accounts. I learned the dark web pretty well and make international connections. So whenever there's a data breach? Those are my boys and the people I buy profile or accounts from. The people I buy work from charge for these. Hasim paid for them. The higher the credit line, the better the info, the more guaranteed it would hit—the more expensive. And sometimes it didn't work. No refunds in this life. Taking an L can hurt more then just the store shutting you down. At one point we were paying $10,000 for sure shot, airtight, A1 profiles."

She exhaled, then kept going.

"We were good. Three million saved in cash, a few million in crypto currency and cash scattered in different bank accounts. Big house, a dog and I was even doing yoga. Two BMWs. We were happy."

She zoned out, forgot to pass the joint, then snapped back and continued.

"But Hasim got greedy. His friend found some overseas crypto wallet from Hong Kong they thought they could crack—had like twenty million in it. He became obsessed. Day in day out they ran software and tweaked programs to crack this wallet. I begged him to leave it alone. They wouldn't. And eventually... they got in."

She finally handed me the joint.

"I was already scared when they pulled the money and scattered it through a bunch of wallets, trying to hide the transaction. They could've taken a little. But no—they emptied it. The entire 20 million. And then we sat like sitting ducks."

She stared at the pool, jaw tight.

"Months pass. His boys start buying Lambos, Porsches, Ferraris. Living loud as hell. Then people started dying. TuoTuo was killed leaving a dice game. They beat him so badly it was a closed casket funeral. Ricardo was into racing but somehow was run off the highway. Each one closer and closer. And then..."

She paused.

"I woke up to being dragged out of bed by my hair in the middle of the night. They had Hasim tied up and duct-taped in the damn living room. And these weren't regular dudes—these were stone-faced Asian men, armed to the teeth, and one of them had a whole sword. Like, an actual sword. For what?
Why the hell did they need a sword in our living room?" She giggled then continued.
"They were screaming about their money, spit flying, guns waving. Long story short—I grabbed the laptop and started transferring our portion back to them. When they made the split 5 ways it was only five million each.
Only. They pistol-whipped me every time the screen lagged, every time I blinked too slow. By the end of it, they made me empty everything we had into their crypto wallet.
And then, on the way out, the meanest one turned around and shot Hasim dead-center in the forehead. No hesitation. My scream didn't even feel human; it felt like my soul got ripped out through my mouth. Another one kicked me in the stomach so hard the world went black for a second. And right before they walked out, someone lit the damn house on fire.

I didn't know what to do, run to Hasim or run for my life. I had to accept he was gone and snap out of it. I kissed him all over his face, grabbed whatever I could reach, and tore out the front door. Everything burned. Everything.
I couldn't answer questions. How we got money, who would want to hurt us. I Couldn't explain any of it. So I disappeared. I had a little left in offshore accounts, the money I had stashed and borrowed the rest. To survive, I started selling exotic weed to rich people and Hollywood weirdos. One of my clients happened to be hanging around Biggs. He recognized me from work I did with Hasim, and we started talking money. That was six months ago. I've been trying to rebuild ever since."

I sat there, stunned—my jaw locked, my brain frozen.

"So… are those guys still after you?" was all I managed to get out.

"I honestly don't know," she said quietly. "They left me alive, but they killed him. I hope didn't inherit his debt. I'm just trying to get my footing back. And that… is why you're here."

I braced myself. Here came the bomb.

"In all honesty, we need more people on our team to maximize profit," she said, eyes softening. "Biggs asked if I knew someone who needed money—someone we could trust. Before you say anything, let me finish. We spend top dollar for the numbers we get. Worst case? The card declines. That's it. No cops. No charges. I've tested it for six months before I even called you."

"So why did we have to rush out of the hotels earlier?" I asked.

"Because sometimes the transaction approves at first, then declines while processing. When that happens, we dip before anyone comes looking."

"I don't know, Maddox… This feels like stealing. I don't wanna end up in jail."

"A'Maya," she said, leaning in, "nobody's going to jail. And nobody's stealing. This is a middle finger to the big banks. The system. They reverse everything anyway."

"What about the people the charges get reversed from?" I asked.

She went silent. Then: "Let God sort them out. You in?"

Her brows lifted, that reckless, fearless look all over her face. Something in me twisted. This didn't feel right. But I needed money. Just a little. Enough to get on my feet, grab some clothes, get back home, and bow out gracefully. That's what I told myself.

I still needed to call my mom. I still needed stability. I still needed something to pull me out of the hole I'd been living in.

What do I really have to lose?

(Oh, I'd learn the answer soon enough.)

"I'm in, Maddox... if it's what you say it is."

She looked at me with those tired, ocean-dark blue eyes, and for some reason I trusted her. I still trusted her.

"It is, A'Maya. I swear." She wrapped her arms around me, warm and grateful.

I wanted to believe her.

I wanted to believe every lie.

But life doesn't always give us what we want.

CHAPTER 6

Walking back into the house, I see Ice in the living room with his girl.

"Aye, y'all hungry?" he asks.

Without answering, we sink onto the couch and glance at the takeout menu.

Biggs walks in, no shirt on, a towel draped around his neck.

"Hey y'all," he exhales, wiping his face. "Order P.F. Chang's—like, cater-style. Hey, 1 Chance, you think you can get some girls over here? Let's have some company tonight—I'm feeling good." He flashes that damn grin of his.

I roll my eyes inside my head.

"I'll do my best," I reply.

"You got that large following on IG. Pull some baddies in. Shiiiid. Maddox, hit up those video vixen chicks too," Biggs laughs.

"Ok, I'm on it," Maddox says, fingers flying over her phone. Her long, expensive nails click across the glass like rapid-fire percussion.

Ice whispers something to his girl and leads her to another room. I grab my phone, start DMing followers in the LA area, hoping for a decent crowd. To my surprise, the responses flood in. Mansion parties in Hollywood aren't a novelty—any day of the week is fair game. Rappers, influencers, and all sorts of entertainment hangers-on start RSVPing instantly.

I turn to Maddox. "I've got a few guys in the industry—can they pull up too?"

"Yeah, but keep the men minimal. Females are easier to control," she says without looking up.

"Wait, what do you mean by video vixens?" I ask, green and naive. Who is this girl, and where did my friend go?

"You'll see soon enough. What are you wearing tonight?" Her question throws me off. I hadn't thought that far ahead—everything is moving so fast I still feel jet-lagged from my flight.

"Umm, I didn't think about it yet… I could check my—"

"Tati's on her way to take you to the Beverly Center. You'll get fresh and grab some inventory," Maddox cuts me off, calm as ever.

Tati? Beverly Center? Inventory? My brain stutters. "How much am I supposed to get today?"

"Whatever you feel like. Tati's a professional—she'll show you the ropes."

I barely have time to process before Maddox says, "She's outside now."

I stare at the door. Forty-eight seconds feel like a lifetime. She stops typing, looks up, eyes locked on mine, almost impatient.

"You good?"

I stand, grab my bag off the chair, and head for the door.

"Oh, wait," Maddox blurts, digging in her Gucci computer bag. She pulls out a driver's license and hands it to me. Roberta Sanchez? 43? Winnetka, Illinois? I'm twenty-eight! Whose name is this with my picture?

Then she hands me five credit cards, each matching the ID. I didn't sign up for any of this.

"What the hell, Maddox?" I snap, disbelief dripping from my voice.

Her cold stare doesn't waver. "Do you want in or not?"

I think of my apartment back in Brooklyn, my mom's constant nagging about my failures, my life in pieces.

I take the cards, wordless, and walk out.

Outside, a white Nissan Altima with dark tinted windows waited. The reggae thump carried across the cobblestone driveway. I opened the door and was hit with a cloud of high-grade smoke. For a second, I thought the car was on fire. But this is California—the state that legalized ganja, and everyone partakes.

The door shut behind me, and the car shot forward like we were racing in the Indy 500. I couldn't take my eyes off her. Tati was stunning. Long, wavy black hair spilling down her back, skin golden-brown like desert sand, hazelnut eyes, high cheekbones, a nose that looked like Walt Disney sketched it.

"What's good? I'm Tati," she shouted over the bass. One hand on the wheel, the other holding a joint.

"1 Chance," I said, deciding not to use my real name.

"I like that. In life, you only got one chance," she said, taking another hit and passing it to me.

"You smoke?" I asked.

"Not right now. Maybe later. Don't want to be paranoid," I replied.

"Nah, I hear you. I need it for my nerves," she affirmed.

The ride lasted about thirty minutes. She told me her story: 23, chasing the finer things, an older married boyfriend who plays for the Dodgers, a broken home, but Maddox had taken her under her wing. I couldn't help but feel sorry for her. She didn't know the life she was throwing herself into—but who was I to judge?

Ten minutes from the mall, Tati switched into work mode. She broke down the plan, told me where to meet if anything went wrong, and handed me a cell phone for communication. Maddox was right—she was laser-focused.

Every step she described, I saw in my mind. She parked near the exit. We put on sunglasses and walked into the mall. My heart thumped louder than the music that still pulsed in her car.

As soon as we entered, we split. Stores everywhere. I had no idea where to go. Panic clawed at me. My mother was right, I might be a loser.

Then my phone buzzed. A text from Maddox. Seeing her name spiked my nerves. "Don't worry, A'maya baby. Please be calm. You got this. Breathe. If you act like it's you, you're good."

This mind-reading thing was getting out of hand. I texted back: "Ok Maddie. I got this."

I closed my eyes, took deep breaths, and opened them like I was about to command a throne. Right in front of me, Roberto Cavil. My heart jumped. I straightened my back, forced Queen Elizabeth-level confidence, and started looking at items.

"Can I help you?" a man asked from behind.

My heart nearly exploded.

"No," I muttered, and bolted out of the store. Abort mission.

I walked over to the banister and peered down at the lower floor. Tati strolled past, three big Bloomingdale's bags dangling from her left arm, a vanilla ice cream cone in her right hand, which she was happily licking. Get yourself together, A'Maya! I told myself. My eyes locked on Saint Laurent. Maybe it was competitiveness, maybe a twinge of jealousy but seeing Tati fueled my ambition.

I headed straight for the shoes. I didn't check the price, just asked for my size. I remembered the sizes Tati said sold well, so I grabbed one pair for me, one pair for them.

Then I walked through the store, picking up men's shirts and shoes. By the time I reached the register, I'd made a small mountain of merchandise, unsure if it was too much.

The older cashier, who reminded me of Richard Gere, smiled and announced the total: "29,734.86." I forced my face into a neutral mask and handed over one of the cards.

"Do you have your I.D., Miss...?" the neatly dressed man asked, reading from the card. "Sanchez?"

Play it cool, A'Maya. My pep talk wasn't helping. My heart thumped in my chest as I handed him the I.D Maddox had made for me. He scanned it, then looked up. "43? Wow, you look young."

Black don't crack, I muttered under my breath, trying to stay calm.

CLICK. The register drawer popped open, the receipt started printing, and I exhaled a sigh so deep it nearly took me out.

"Do you need any help to your car, ma'am?" the man asked. I glanced at his name tag for the first time—Roger. My anxiety spiked again. "No, handsome, I got it. Thank you," I said, smiling warmly as I scooped up the five big bags and hurried toward the exit.

I kept glancing over my shoulder, making sure no one was coming from either direction. Nothing. I walked on, trying to steady my racing heart.

The MCM store came into view, and I finally caught my breath. The New Yorker in me had always loved their vintage print. My family could never afford anything from that brand—the one rappers and drug dealers had made iconic. Well, let's try to get one today.

I walked into the store with a different kind of confidence, the kind that sits on your hips and swings with your steps. Those bags felt like proof I finally belonged in the rooms I used to window-shop from. I went straight for the medium Stark backpack, grabbed the matching bucket hat, and topped it with a wool beanie in the same print. For a second I forgot why I was even here. The mission drifted off and that old childhood ache of wanting nice things tugged at me.

I snapped out of it, doubled back, and grabbed another full set for the pot. A backpack, bucket hat, beanie—and added a belt plus a few women's pieces.

"8,421.98," the cashier announced.

Tati's voice rang in my head: Never use the same card twice.

I slid the first card deep into my purse, pulled out the blue credit card, and handed it over with the I.D already in my palm so he wouldn't even ask.

CLICK. POP. Zzzzit zzzzzit zzzzzit.

The longer the receipt printed, the more my nerves sank back into my stomach where they belonged.

Three more cards. Three more stores.

By the time I hit the last one, I couldn't believe how easy it had become. The bags on my arms felt like armor—like I was playing a role and winning at it. Almost $100,000 today. One hundred thousand dollars.

My head spun.

My heart kicked.

My life tilted.

I'm about to get fresh tonight.

I did the math fast—if the split was what Maddox said... I was walking away with something like $25,000. Twenty-five racks. In a day.

I texted Tati that I was done. She replied instantly already at the meeting point.

I hustled out of the mall, excitement tripping over caution with every step. The trunk of the Altima was already stuffed by the time I got there, so I stacked everything in the backseat until Tati couldn't see out the rear window.

She peeled out onto Beverly Blvd, reggae thumping from her half-rolled-down window. The second she hit a red light, I let out a scream I didn't even know lived inside me. Pure adrenaline, my hands in the air, my head shaking back and forth like I'd just been reborn.

I couldn't believe what I just did.

On the drive back, I finally hit the joint she passed me. The sun dipped behind the buildings on Sunset Blvd, throwing gold all over the city. The early evening air was warm but had that soft California cool brushing against my skin.

When we pulled up to the house, it looked like a luxury car dealership exploded on the driveway—Lambos, Maybachs, Bentleys, foreigns I didn't even know the name of.

Before we even reached the door, three young Black girls rushed out to grab all the bags from the car. Tati and I split our personal items from the pot and handed the rest off.

We reached the estate and pulled inside. Maddox stood in the doorway in a sleeveless Balmain crocodile dress, holding a glass of wine and wearing a face full of makeup like she woke up in glam. She graces her way to the car.

"These the things you're keeping for you?" she asked, smiling.

I nodded, still wearing the MCM bucket hat I'd just bought.

"Okay, let's go see what you got."

I walked into the room she gave me and dropped the bags. Everything inside was modern and grey, perfectly neat—too neat, like no one had ever lived in here . Maddox went through the bags, and her face fell.

"I gotta go shopping with you next time, just us," she sighed. "We need a high-end look. Just because it's name brand doesn't make it fashion."

Embarrassment shot through me.

"Okay, but in my defense, you asked if I had something for a house party tonight," I said, confused. "And I don't even know the attire because... I don't know what's going on."

"You're absolutely right, A'Maya," Maddox admitted. "Tomorrow we'll have a day to ourselves and go into full detail."

She pulled me into a hug.

"I'm so happy you're here."

But when she let go, she stayed close—almost too close. Like she wanted me to really see her. And I did. The lines around her mouth. The makeup settling into edges that weren't there a few years ago. The exhaustion , the chemicals and the speed of her life creeping up on her twenty eight-year-old face.

She drew a deep breath, turned toward the door, then paused.

"Good job today," she said softly. "Get dressed, we got company."

Then she disappeared behind the heavy wooden door.

I showered quick, put on my MCM outfit with a black fitted tee, black jeans, suede Timbs, a face of makeup, and my fake jewelry that gleamed like the real thing. Sprayed on 7 pumps of the YSL perfume I bought earlier.

I scanned the room, estimating what I kept.

Maybe $15,000 in merch.

So if the day's total was around $80,000... that meant $20,000 for me.

I'm up, baby.

Feeling myself, I walked down the hallway. The 808s vibrated through the walls, brushing against my skin. Conversations floated everywhere, a low hum under the music.

Biggs was the first person I saw, walking toward me with that same damn grin. Fresh haircut, lips still ashy, Prada sneakers, a Burberry button-down, and diamonds flashing like a light show every time he moved.

"You gon' hop on the DJ equipment?" he asked. "A lot of these people here 'cause of you!" He drawled it out, slow and deliberate. I scanned the room, trying to process how they had pulled this off so fast. A catered table was set up with everything off the P.F. Chang menu. A bar glistened under soft lighting, and a DJ set with flashing lights spun tracks outside by the pool.

"Hell yeah! This is lit! I'll grab some food and hop on!" I shouted, excitement clawing at my chest.

The place was packed with girls straight out of music videos, laughing, sipping, and grazing on small plates. I grabbed a little of everything, even if I wasn't planning to eat it, and began a slow walk through the crowd, trying to figure out who was who. The muscle men, the athletes, the obvious gangsters and scam artists.

Ice sat at a table with this Russian girl, so I drifted that way. Ice's hair was slicked back so smooth it looked like vinyl. A slim mustache and a tight chinstrap beard lined his face perfectly. Black Armani tee, black cargo shorts, Chuck Taylors, and jewelry that gleamed like Biggs'. His girl wore a black dress. A very stunning but cold woman. Her sharp, Ice blue eyes and bone straight dark red hair stood out the most to me. We didn't talk, I just kept people-watching.

C-list celebrities popped pills, snorted lines off playing cards. Girls were stripping, diving into the pool mid-laugh.

Sabrina "the creamer"approached from the kitchen area.

"Hey, A'Maya."

I froze.

"1 Chance," I blurted.

"Huh?"

"Call me 1 Chance."

"Oh, okay... can I just do Chance?" she smiled warmly.

She motioned to two people behind her. "This is Kinky Kitty and Paul the Pounder. We just left a set. I wanted them to party with us" She tries to yell over the music.

Kitty's European beauty hit first—dark eyes, messy bun, pleather dress so tight it barely contained her curves. Paul was steroidal, tanned too much, high on whatever vice of the week, wide blue eyes scanning the room. He nodded to everyone around, moving slightly offbeat to the music.

"Nice to meet you," I shouted over the beat. He nodded, then leaned sideways: "If you need ANYTHING, let me know." I shook his hand, nodding in polite confusion. I shook Kitty's hand, rested my hand on Sabrina's shoulder, then made my way to the DJ booth.

Maddox was there, off to the side by the speakers, looking impossibly elegant. Magazine-perfect. She jumped slightly as I approached, spilling some of her drink.

"You're going to DJ?!" she shouted, bouncing.

"Yes, I'll get on when he's done," I said.

"Fuck that, he's done!" she rolled her eyes, rushing to whisper in the DJ's ear. He waved me over.

"Nice to finally meet you, 1 Chance. Huge fan, I follow you!" DJ Pendulum yelled, shaking my hand before passing me the headphones and walking off. It wasn't financial, but in that moment, I felt rich. Seen. Appreciated.

I grabbed the mic, scrolled through his software, found the right track, and let it rip.

"Yes, yes, y'all! It's your girl, DJ 1 Chance! If you came to party, say HELL YEAH!"

The roar of the crowd hit me like electricity. The first drop—Trap Queen by Fetty Wap—sent the room into a frenzy. I kept the energy rolling for three straight hours, Maddox and Tati fetching drinks whenever mine ran dry, sticking close to watch me rock the crowd. People came up, filming, snapping photos. My phone buzzed incessantly in my back pocket.

Finally, I answered:

"So you go party in California and forget about your mother?"

My chest sank. I'd been meaning to call, but never at a moment like this.

"Ma, it's a three-hour difference, plus I'm working right now," I yelled over the music.

"I'm praying for you, mija. I don't know what kind of work you're doing, but I am praying for you."

"OK, Ma," I groaned internally. This is exactly why I haven't been calling.

"I'm busy doing a party right now."

I grabbed the mic. "Aye, y'all, my mom's on the phone back in Brooklyn! Can y'all say hey, Ma?!"

The drunken roar of the crowd—Hey Ma!—made my cheeks burn.

"Ok, mija, have fun. But please be safe. Oh my God, I have to pray everyone at that party gets home safely. I love you, take care, and don't forget to pray, my baby."

"Ok, mommy, I love you too. I'll call you tomorrow."

I threw on the next song, but my mother's call kept replaying in my head. Does she feel something as a mother? What kind of work am I doing?

No time for that now, my tequila-fueled brain told itself. Stay focused. Have fun.

I watched Ice and Biggs work the room all night from my DJ booth perch. Ice moved from girl to girl, and one out of every four or five exchanged numbers. Biggs? He shared information with almost everyone he spoke to. My paranoid side whispered, Is this a party or a recruitment ceremony?

I looked over at Maddox, Tati dancing next to her, the crowd pulsing around them, and my doubts multiplied. Was I just a pawn in something bigger? Was my friend really on my side?

Luckily, by the time my thoughts started killing my mood, the party was winding down. I exchanged numbers with local DJs and a few people who wanted to book me for gigs. I had completely forgotten I invited Brian, and his text popped in: "Just landed in Thailand on business. I'll be back in 3 days. Let's get lunch."

Butterflies hit me unexpectedly. Not sure if it was him or the intoxication. Either way, I was drained. Pushing through the stragglers leaving the house, snippets of praise floated toward me: "Good job tonight, 1 Chance," or the occasional "What's up, 1 Chance?"

This felt amazing. Finally, I saw the power my followers could have. New York felt stagnant, but out here, I realized the path I was on could either elevate me—or destroy me.

I locked myself in my room, leaned against the door, and exhaled. Okay. Stack the money. Leave before this becomes a lifestyle. No room for mistakes. No room for compromise. Promises get broken, even when no one's at fault. But this one—I had to keep.

CHAPTER 7

I woke up to the smell of bacon and something sweet. The Versace robe I kept draped on the computer chair felt luxurious over my silk pajamas. Slipping on the hotel slippers I had stashed, I made my way to the kitchen.

Voices ,more than had been traveling with us so far, echoed around the space. At the stove was Doll Baby, one of the biggest vixens on social media with like three million followers. Black lace bra and panty set, high heels, slim and athletic but with curves. She's Jamaican and Japanese, with a lightly tanned flawless face, but I could see the cost of the profession written in her every move.

"Good morning, love," she smiled, flipping eggs with one hand and a spatula in the other.

"Hey, Doll Baby," I replied like I knew her already.

At the back table looked like the United Nations of vixens surrounding Ice. His Russian girl, a 4'11 chubby-faced girl with a coffee complexion and thick brick house build, a smokey-eyed Filipino with an athletic frame, and a Hispanic girl who reminded me of Tati.

"Good morning, lil sis," Ice toasted with a grin, gold teeth glinting in the morning light. I returned the salute as I headed for the oversized coffee mugs. Damn, this headache needed an Advil.

Another vixen passed by, barely clothed. "You hungry, sugar? I made you a plate," Doll Baby called. I thanked her, grabbed my food, and went to the pool, taking a seat under the umbrella. Three girls of different nationalities swam nude, while Biggs lounged, sunbathing with a cigar in hand.

Where are you, A'maya? I asked myself.

I bit into the bacon, then my pancake, when Maddox appeared. "Where's your glass?" she asked, pouring champagne in front of me. "Tati! Orange juice!" She turned back to me, sliding a pair of dark sunglasses onto my face. "It's fresh-squeezed, delicious. Here, put these on."

"Good morning, Maddox," I muttered, mouth full.

She stretched in her sheer robe, bra and underwear showing underneath. "Hey, 1 Chance."

"What the hell is going on here? Every day it's a new dimension. Now I'm at the Playboy Mansion?" I laughed nervously.

"You live once, right? Gotta enjoy every minute," she said, lighting a cigarette, taking a long drag, exhaling. "Look at this house. We've always wanted this."

"You don't get scared? Nervous about getting locked up?" I asked, innocently.

"I don't even think like that," she said, sipping champagne. "I forbid you to. I've already lived the worst part. They killed my man in front of me. Burned my house down. Not much else left." Another pull of smoke. "So I push it every day. Hasim showed me you can't take this with you. We can leave anytime. No rewards in playing it safe."

Her words made sense but saddened me. My mom played it safe, kept her head down, and went to work every day. Twenty-five years later, she was still in the same apartment, at the same job.

Tati poured orange juice into our champagne glasses, fixing herself a mimosa before joining the table. Doll Baby followed with a plate of freshly cut fruit. We ate in silence.

I was getting used to discomfort, to always being ready to jet. We had stayed over 24 hours and now I sat at the edge of my seat, anticipating the next move.

Maddox finished eating and lit another cigarette. After the first exhale, she began: "Ok, girls. Today's Friday. We're hitting different banks. Biggs will have new IDs for everyone by the time we get dressed. Doll Baby, you're with Malik. Tati, you're with Sabrina. Me and 1 Chance are together today."

"Who's A'maya?" Tati asked between bites.

"Oh, my bad. 1 Chance," Maddox said, exhaling smoke as she rose. "Get dressed, ladies. Wheels up in 45. Dress to impress. Makeup, please." She waltzed away.

A bank? What the hell are we doing now?

I did my best to look exquisite, though frustration bubbled beneath the surface. My wardrobe was casual hip-hop, not exactly ready for high-end fashion.

When I opened the front door, three SUVs waited, drivers standing in front of each. Maddox appeared behind me, tapping my shoulder and gesturing for me to follow her into the first truck.

"Maddox, I don't know about any bank. I can't—"

"Shhhh," she interrupted, glancing at the driver. "That's not for us today. We're going to Rodeo Drive so you can dress the part."

The driver pulled off, and I sat quietly, taking in the scenery. Rows of mansions with lawns more manicured than me. People jogging without a care, million-dollar cars whizzing past. We passed the iconic Beverly Hills sign.

"I'll call you when we're ready," Maddox told the driver as we hopped out in front of Louis Vuitton.

Inside, she commanded every store. She styled me like her muse, pulling clothes from racks with a confidence that sucked the air from the room. Her deep blue eyes were trustworthy, magnetic, and each movement exuded power. At every counter, she carried herself like royalty, champagne and free samples flowing in her wake.

Once done, she called the driver, handed off the bags, and we stopped at a restaurant for a quick bite. Alone at a quiet table, she finally opened up.

"A'maya, you're not going to do certain jobs the other girls do. I must keep my promise to keep you safe. When I say the 'lick' for the day, I don't want the others asking why you don't have to do certain things."

She slid an envelope across the table. "Here's twelve grand from yesterday."

I frowned. "That's... a little off from the calculations you told me."

"Baby, do you think today was free? That was real money. 100% legit. I can't be outside playing."

I wasn't thrilled, but I couldn't be mad. This was more than I could have asked for.

"Okay, I appreciate it, Maddox. Next time, let me know. I could have taken it a little easier," I joked.

"Oh, you thought I was tricking on you? Hahaha. Joke's on you," she laughed, taking a sip of her drink.

We ate appetizers, took a few shots, and she shared her plan and vision. I believed her, even if I hated the way she had to go about it.

Back at the house, the front door opened to chaos: topless women pillow-fighting, leaping from couch to couch, while Ice smoked on a stool by the pool. Loud hip-hop music blasted from the television. I nodded at Ice and headed to my room.

Laying out my new wardrobe, I took it all in. I'd never had this many high-end items or this much cash at once. Since landing, I hadn't spent a dime, so I was up $12,900. Bills, my mom's rent, and stack for myself. At this rate ill be papered up if I stay just a month, especially at the pace they worked.

A light knock at the door announced Maddox, wine glass in one hand, rolling a dark gray suitcase with the other.

"You've got a ton of new stuff, you may have to move at a moment's notice," she giggled, pushing the shell toward me. She left without another word.

Passing the kitchen, I watched Baby Doll prep food for the grill. Even with her history—Lil Wayne, Drake, The Weeknd videos—she radiated a grounded, positive energy. Each girl I'd met had a childlike innocence, and Baby Doll led the pack.

I wasn't thrilled, but I couldn't be mad. This was more than I could have asked for.

"Okay, I appreciate it, Maddox. Next time, let me know. I could have taken it a little easier," I joked.

"Oh, you thought I was tricking on you? Hahaha. Joke's on you," she laughed, taking a sip of her drink.

We ate appetizers, took a few shots, and she shared her plan and vision. I believed her, even if I hated the way she had to go about it.

Back at the house, the front door opened to chaos: topless women pillow-fighting, leaping from couch to couch, while Ice smoked on a stool by the pool. Loud hip-hop music blasted from the television. I nodded at Ice and headed to my room.

Laying out my new wardrobe, I took it all in. I'd never had this many high-end items or this much cash at once. Since landing, I hadn't spent a dime, so I was up $12,900. Bills, my mom's rent, and stack for myself. At this rate ill be papered up if I stay just a month, especially at the pace they worked.

A light knock at the door announced Maddox, wine glass in one hand, rolling a dark gray suitcase with the other.

"You've got a ton of new stuff, you may have to move at a moment's notice," she giggled, pushing the shell toward me. She left without another word.

Passing the kitchen, I watched Baby Doll prep food for the grill. Even with her history—Lil Wayne, Drake, The Weeknd videos—she radiated a grounded, positive energy. Each girl I'd met had a childlike innocence, and Baby Doll led the pack.

I met Maddox back at the breakfast table. She turned the space into her office, typing away on her mini computer. Tap, tap, tap.
I scrolled my iPhone, entertained myself quietly.

Within minutes, Tati and Maliak joined us, Biggs not far behind.
"Wells Fargo was easy, but not one damn Bank of America would let me cash a check. Talking about accounts, blah, blah, blah," Tati asserted,
passing six envelopes to Maddox.

"Fifteen thousand in each one," Maliak confirmed.
Biggs watched silently from near the BBQ grill.
Maddox counted out thirty thousand, handing ten grand apiece.

I did my best to hide my astonishment at the sheer flow of money and how organized everything was. Biggs walked over slowly, inhaled from his cigar, and exhaled in that deep southern drawl.

"After we eat, pack up. We're moving to a new location."
Then he drifted into the kitchen. Moving again?
How do they live like this?

CHAPTER 8

We tore into Doll Baby's homemade cheeseburgers, baked beans, and corn on the cob, laughing and enjoying the evening. My bags were already packed, so I joined Tati for a joint as everyone gathered their things. Ice loaded his bags into Malik's trunk. Three of the girls he had with him followed suit, piling into Malik's fully pimped-out impala. Green and blue, chrome-spiked rims, a sound system you could hear down the block.

Doll Baby, Maddox, and I hopped into a waiting truck with Biggs up front. It was 10:39 p.m.—late to be moving—but I followed their lead. The ride was short, ending in Bel-Air. I'd only heard of this town from Fresh Prince of Bel-Air. The mega-mansion waiting for us was perched on a cul-de-sac, high above the city with insane views.

It looked like it was made of glass. Four floors, Italian kitchen with black counters, a dramatic waterfall island, a glass-enclosed wine cabinet. Double-sided fireplace in the living room, heated marble floors, mirrored walls, an entire wall of glass opening to a deck and infinity pool. Crystal chandeliers, priceless art, Japanese-inspired trees—everything screamed opulence.

We moved in single file upstairs to pick bedrooms. I prayed we could stay longer than one night. I chose the room farthest from the stairs and headed straight to the shower.

Around midnight, I heard voices. Descending the dark marble and glass stairs, I found Ice and Biggs playing pool while some of the girls played spades by the fireplace. Jazz music played softly—an oddly classy touch in the midst of this chaos. Maddox sat by the pool, feet in the water, soaking in the view.

I kicked off my hotel slippers and joined her.

"Hey, Maddy the Baddy. How are you feeling?" I nudged her shoulder lightly.

She smiled. "I'm tired, A'maya... or 1 Chance... or Chance... or girl, whatever you want me to call you," she joked.

"Chance works. But seriously, you tired? Talk to me."

"I don't know what I'm doing, Chance," I admitted. "I think I like 'Chance.' Haha. Back in college, I lost my way, got tied up in this lifestyle, and now I'm chasing a ghost. Hasim and I didn't have to do these kinds of jobs. I just know how to navigate the black market, how to use Bitcoin for transactions. He knew how to get the money. I'm valuable to any team—it just depends on the game they're playing. Biggs is cool, but I don't know if I like how we move."

Like a mind reader, she anticipated my worry. "You don't have anything to worry about. This is the whole game we're playing, not the players in it. Banks, malls—that's his game. I just know how to find safe profiles, but those are expensive. That's why he wants a team. More people out at once, more money made." She took a long drag of her cigarette.

"I want to stack up enough, relocate, and figure something else out," I admitted.

"What's your goal number?" she asked.

"That's the thing—I don't know yet. Maybe I need to figure that out first, then work toward it."

She exhaled slowly. "Cause I'll be honest. I like the money, the thrill, the perks—but I, too, want to stack up and call it a night."

"So... you're going to leave me?" I joked, trying to mask the tension.

She whipped her head to meet my eyes. "No, Maddox. I mean maybe we set a goal and boogie together or something. This isn't my future, and I feel a little guilty."

Her warm, motherly look softened me. "I get it. I'll wrap my head around it in the next few days and get back to you."

"Get back to her on what?" Biggs interrupted, appearing from behind with a pool stick in hand.

Quick on her feet, Maddox replied, "She wanted to go sightseeing and asked what days we didn't have any motion. Damn, Biggs, I wasn't ear-hustling what you and Ice were yapping about!"

"Yeah, aight. Only day we have off is tomorrow for the next couple of days. Run around town if you want," he shot back with a stern look.

"Biggs baby, we work together, but please don't talk to me like you're my man or my boss," Maddox asserted sweetly but firmly.

"I'm your man and your boss, gotdamn it," he quipped.

"Gotdamn, Maddox, why you gotta be so cold?"

"'Cause you keep playing with me," she fired back, taking a long drag of her cigarette.

He laughed and walked back to his pool game. I couldn't help but feel proud of Maddox for the way she handled Biggs. From that alone, I could tell she didn't let anyone play with her.

"Girl, you can't give them an inch in these streets. Speak up the first time, because by the second time, the sharks already smell blood," she vented.

"Ok, so what's on the agenda tomorrow if we're taking off?" I asked.

"You see this house!? Another party! We're gonna charge the door, put you on the flyer, and Biggs swears he's getting celebrities again. I'll hire the caterer. Hit your people up again. $75 per person, top-shelf open bar, food, games, whatever else."

"Ok... how am I getting paid? A'maya and 1 Chance are two different entities," I reminded her.

"Ok, ok, I like that. Finally speaking up," she said, smiling. I felt proud of myself for the first time this trip.

"How much do you normally get paid?" she asked.

"How many people y'all expecting?" I countered.

"The max is 400 before the fire marshal shows up."

Quick math in my head. "$3,500," I replied.

"Sold! Come to my room, I'll pay you now," Maddox shouted as she got up from the pool.

I followed her to her room. The walls were half window, half wall, and the balcony had a French-style tub overlooking the hills. Maddox counted out $4,000 from her stack of hundreds in her Louis Vuitton purse.

"I threw in a tip. Wanna watch a movie? There's a theater downstairs!" she yelped.

Exhausted but not wanting to disappoint her, I smiled. "Let's go."

She grabbed a blanket, her YSL purse, and ran down the hall, yelling, "Tati! Baby Doll! Let's watch a mooooovie!"

We all met in the plush, dimly lit movie theater with enormous seats. Baby Doll brought big bowls of popcorn, and Biggs chose Green Book. By the time I finished my popcorn and curled up under the cashmere blanket, I was out cold within ten minutes.

The sound of a sharp voice jolted me awake.

"Bitch, don't play with me!"

SLAP!

I shot up. The theater chair had been more comfortable than my bed at home. People were rushing out, and I followed, heart pounding. Ice was in the living room, sweat dripping, hair disheveled, rage etched into his face, fist wailing on one of the girls from breakfast.

The small brown-skinned girl from the other house was crouched, lip bleeding, face slightly swollen grunting with each blow. Biggs rushed between them as Maddox and Tati helped her up.

"Biggs, let me go! She's playing with my money!" Ice shouted.

"Not in front of the girls, Ice. You're drunk, man. Take ya ass to bed!" Biggs whispered firmly.

"She gotta go, Biggs! Kick her out! Right now! She's bad luck!" Ice roared.

Biggs stayed composed. "Ice, my brother, it's 3-something in the morning. We can't have a pretty sister walking these streets now." That grin again. "We have plenty of space in here. Let..." he turned to the girl.

"Pepsi," she murmured.

Biggs grinned. "Let Pepsi stay the night, and we take care of this tomorrow, my brother. Please."

Ice exhaled sharply, then muttered, "Fine. But if I see her again, I'm tearing her head off!" He gulped his cocktail and walked to his other girls.

Biggs rubbed the girl's shoulder. "Y'all make Pepsi comfortable. Maddox, make sure she's all right. You're safe. My brother's mad, but we gonna make it right."

I began seeing the chess moves Biggs made—how he treats one man's trash as another man's treasure, how he recruits the girls Ice discards.

I wanted to pick his brain, but we had barely interacted. Now seemed like the time.

"Let me bust ya ass in a game of pool before you head to bed, old man," I joked.

"I ain't old, and you ain't busting my ass. Let's go, shorty!" he replied.

"Rack 'em," he demanded, chalking his stick.

The atmosphere was unreal. I asked, "Where y'all from, Biggs?"

"Solids. All over Ohio, shorty. Cleveland, Cincinnati, Dayton..." He trailed off, sinking another ball.

"You getting money, man. Thanks for letting me get some paper with y'all," I buttered him up.

"Yeah, Maddox said you solid. We ain't been working together long, but that white girl? One of the coldest women I ever met. Y'all knew each other from back east, huh?" he asked, pocketing another ball.

"Yeah, boarding school days," I said.

"How old you?"

"28. Same as Maddox. You?"

"44, going on 45 next year," he replied, slamming the 8-ball in.

"Got any kids?"

"Yea, three. Two boys, a baby girl. Baby mama back home trippin'. May fly her and the girls out here to work a few days," he grinned, matter-of-fact.

"Be happy we wasn't betting!" he joked, laying down his stick.

"I didn't even get to play," I whined playfully.

"My point. I like you, 1 Chance. You mad cool, lil sis," he said, that damn grin again.

"Thanks, Biggs. You too. I'm gonna head to bed. See you in the morning."

CHAPTER 9

Ahh... the smell of bacon slips under my nose like my own personal aroma alarm clock. I slide into my Versace robe and head downstairs, still half-hunting for that YSL perfume I swear was on my dresser last night. Whatever. I follow the food.

Baby Doll is in the kitchen, and she went wild this morning: croissants, scrambled eggs, fruit, yogurt, fresh-squeezed OJ, bacon, sausage, biscuits and gravy, grits — the whole Sunday-morning-church-lady spread. I hate how much I love this life. Ice is at the table with sunglasses on like it's a press conference, his icy grill glinting, two girls tucked in on either side. Maddox is outside with Pepsi, both of them dangling their feet in the pool like they don't have a care in the world. As I walk up, I hear the tail end of Pepsi saying, "We're a family... if it didn't work with Ice, you can see what things are like with us. Take the day off. Enjoy the party. Invite your girlfriends. Let's talk tomorrow."

She nods and then notices me behind her.

"Good morning, Chance," she smiles.

I don't remember giving her my name.

"Hey, P," I say, taking the joint she passes me.

The view is ridiculous — sun, mountains, water — and for a second I just breathe it all in. Something this wrong shouldn't feel this right. I hit the joint again, realizing I'm smoking way more than usual. Before my mind drifts too far, my phone vibrates.

Hey beautiful, I just landed. What you getting into today?

Brian.

I ask Maddox if he can come, and she nods between slow, lazy pulls of the joint. I text him the Bel-Air address for the party I'm DJing tonight. Butterflies hit me again. I don't get it. Brian is nowhere near my type. Slim, no real build under those button-ups, glasses, that little academic afro... but he's articulate, respectful, that perfect smile — the opposite of the knuckleheads I've entertained back home.

"You picking my outfit again tonight?" I tease.

"Yes," she snaps her fingers, "Givenchy hoodie, the shorts, the McQueen sneakers. Hair out, makeup cute. Trust me."

"I was joking, but... that outfit actually sounds fire."

"Girl, I do this."

She studies my face. "It's still early. You wanna get some money with Baby Doll before the party? She needs a few dollars."

I think about my day off... then the money.

"Okay."

She already has my profile ready like she knew damn well I'd say yes.

Monica Jenkins. Teaneck, NJ. 38 years old.

Guilt creeps in but I swallow it. Baby Doll is already outside waiting.

She drives a black Ford Explorer with matching tint — quiet, practical. She's older than the rest of us, thirty-four, with a one-year-old daughter back home. No smoking, no nonsense. We head to the Glendale Galleria, and she breaks down the same game plan Tati taught me.

Once we park, it's showtime.

I walk into Bloomingdale's like I own the place. I'm grabbing everything: bags, shoes, clothes — not even counting, just playing the role. The total lands at $11,624.11 and I hand over the card with the calm of a woman who's done this for years.

"Sorry, miss, this card is declined. Do you have another?" the cashier says.

My heart drops straight to hell.

Don't panic.

"That's weird," I say lightly, offering another card while my pulse bangs like African drums. He checks... shakes his head.

"Nope, this one isn't working either."

My sweat turns cold. I want to run, but I keep my face flat.

"Strange... let me call my husband. I'll be right back, Brad." (Thank God for name tags.)

"I'll hold these. It happens all the time with large purchases," he says.

I walk out calm — and take that lesson with me. Never panic. Banks decline big charges every day.

I call Maddox on the burner. She's typing like a hacker in a movie.

"Oh this hoe got alerts on. Hold on, I'm forwarding them. One sec... okay go back in. I fixed it."

I go back.

"You were right, Brad. It was the bank," I smile, handing him the card.

He swipes.

CLICK. POP. ZZZZZIT.

The receipt prints.

I breathe again.

But I'm hungry now. That adrenaline opens up a different kind of appetite. I head to the Apple Store. Eight new iPhones, four top-tier laptops, accessories — all of it.

Total: $21,336.48.

I hand over a fresh card.

"Ma'am, do you have another?"

Of course she asks.

I give her the card that worked last time. She tries it.

"Maybe call your bank, ma'am... it says the card is locked and to call security."

She didn't even mean to let that slip, I can tell. I take the card, nod, stay composed.

As soon as I'm outside, I call Maddox. She doesn't even let me finish — she clicks the line over and tells Baby Doll to get me out of the mall now.

No security in sight, but my heart doesn't care. I speed-walk like hell in heels. Baby Doll is already at the curb with the engine running. I toss the bags in and jump in after them.

We're gone before anyone even realizes there was a problem.

"Girl, what happened!?" Baby Doll slams the gas, weaving through the streets like a bat out of hell. I spill the whole story.

"Yea, that profile is burned. Maddox should've known," she says.

"How?" I ask, heart still hammering.

"If they were texting the girl, she got the first two alerts. Probably shut her cards down. That one that went through? That was your one chance today," she jokes, trying to lighten the tension.

"Aye, don't let it shake you. Happens to the best of us. You got out — that's what matters."

I nod, still feeling my pulse slam against my ribs.

We pull through the gate. Maddox is at the door, wine glass in hand.

"Aww, my baby! Are you okay?" she teases.

"That was scary, Maddox. What if she really called security?"

"What if I could shit gold eggs? Can't worry about what isn't. Be grateful for what is, my friend." She throws her arm over my shoulder and guides me inside.

The house is alive: people everywhere decorating and prepping for the party in a few hours. "There's where you'll be rocking out, Chance," she points to the DJ setup by the pool. I'm still shaken, but Maddox doesn't let me linger. At the top of the stairs, she stops me.

"A'maya. Tighten the fuck up. You had your cherry broken. Don't let it mess up the night. You got paid to kill this party — and that's exactly what you better do, bitch!" Her tone softens into a smile by the end. She's right. And yeah... I should probably be looking at flights to get the hell out of here, too. She ushers me to my room with her usual command: Hurry up.

Downstairs, the house pulses with energy. Beautiful people wall-to-wall. We've blocked the stairs leading to our quarters, but the rest of the house is free game. Sabrina, the creamer, has her movie friends off on the balcony, passing around lines of something. I frown. Such a shame.

Tati catches my eye in the corner, talking to a very pretty girl in a way that makes me pause. It's subtle, different — intimate. I file it away for later.

Biggs is at the bar, surrounded by young girls nearly half his age. Clothes fresh, neat baldy, but can't find any chapstick. Predator? Scumbag? Maybe both. I glare. He catches it, lifts his head, locks eyes with me, and raises his glass. That damn grin. I shiver and wave back with a fake smile.

Maddox is on the balcony by the fireplace, dealing with a muscular, rugged reggaeton artist. Famous, around the globe but I skip that part. He's aggressive; her drunk body resists his hugs and affection. I step closer to intervene, and suddenly Ice blocks my path.

"What's good, Ice?" I ask.

"She likes it like that. Haven't known her long, but this is what they do. Let her be. You try to help, you get cursed out. We've all done it." He slides aside, letting me see. She slaps him lightly, then throws herself into his arms. They kiss, full-on passionate.

"Tele nova shit," I mutter under my breath.

"I'm telling you, kid. First time I saw it, I almost broke his neck. No means no — everywhere. Feel me?" That's rich coming from you, I think.

"But when I try to jump in, she tells us all to mind our business," he recalls.

"And while I got you here... don't like how you beat on Pepsi," his eyes cold now.

"Mind your funky ass business and keep your nose outta mine."

I must've looked hurt because he softens. "My apologies, Chance. You don't mean no harm. But you don't know anything about pimping. That girl? Bad omen. Needs to get away. I keep telling Biggs, but he won't listen."

"Why are you a pimp, Ice?" I ask, staring into those hazel eyes.

"You really wanna know?"

I nod.

"Ok. Tonight. If you're not too tired, we'll build. Now go DJ and stay outta trouble." His gold-toothed smile appears, protective and commanding as he leads me to the booth. Hate this lifestyle, hate the way he chose it, but damn... I can't deny the sexual control he exudes.

"Yes! Yes, party people! Are you ready!?" The crowd erupts. My chest tightens with adrenaline I haven't felt since touring two years ago.

"DJ 1 Choice!" I drop the first bomb effect and unleash the opening track. The night is officially mine.

The crowd went wild, and we had an absolute ball all night. I let drunk girls come up to sing karaoke, and from my vantage point, Biggs and Ice worked the room like two wolves in a chicken coop. A few guys were there too, but they were either famous or just there to bring the sunshine in a bag for anyone who wanted it.

My phone vibrates — a text from Brian: "Don't hate me. Got called into work, can't make it tonight. I'll make it up to you. Have fun!" I shrug and toss it aside.

Some basketball player from a California major team comes up and makes it rain $100 bills on me while I play his favorite tracks. Showing off in front of his friends, he starts a cascade of cash, and one by one, the other players join in, throwing money over the balcony to the floor below. Girls try to come up and twerk for extra cash, but Maddox and Ice act like security, shutting it down immediately.

This night? Hands down the best DJing experience I've ever had. I've traveled the world, but this... this was something else.

"Girl! Who the hell makes $10,000 in tips DJing?" Maddox exclaims later as she gathers up the money with me, counting it after the party. She's even pulled cash that was downstairs while I was still DJing. "Shit," she mutters, wrapping the last stack of hundreds in a rubber band.

"How much you saving up before you leave me?" she asks. I've made over $13,000 today — not even counting the other work. I open my mouth, but she cuts me off. "Biggs and I agree: you're too valuable. Can't have a famous DJ caught up in mall affairs. How about we pay you to DJ and keep the ladies coming to the parties? Let's settle on $5,000 a party."

Relief washes over me. Mall drama aside, this is security. "Yes! Please! God, thank you!" I gush. I'm no scumbag; I still feel guilty about some of the people I've affected, but in this jungle, survival rules.

A knock at the door.

"Y'all decent?"

"Yes!" we answer in unison.

Ice walks in, effortlessly handsome. "Hey, Momma big dollars, can I holla at you?" We all laugh. I tell Maddox I'll be back. She exhales, "Mmm hmm."

Ice and I step onto the deck. We talk until the sun starts to rise. He tells me his story. His family were immigrants from the Philippines. His mother met his father, a black man when she got to America. He manipulated her, using love against her in a strange new land and strung her out on dope. Ice would have to watch his father beat his mother and then send her out on the stroll to make money. His father was a pimp and a small time drug dealer. His mothers side of the family didn't approve of his moms lifestyle and disowned her. His father had a shoot out with the police. He ended up in jail, and Ice, just a kid, had to help his mother survive. By 14, she had him pimping for her. She taught him toughness, how to fight men who tried to cheat her, and he grew up with that monster inside. He was a good student but had to drop out of school eventually.

"The boy who can pimp his own mother," he says, "that's what they called me everywhere. He left Cleveland after his mother died and met Biggs at a dice game over a decade ago. I listened in disbelief. His story is heartbreaking, and now I understand why this is all he knows.

"Ever think of doing something else?" I ask, hope threading my voice.

"What I'm gonna do, A'maya?" he responds honestly.

"What's your real name?"

"I'm a junior. Daddy named me James. I don't like that — Jimmy or JJ — so I went with what a girl called me in school: Ice. And it stuck."

My jaw drops. This boy never had a chance. Everyone in this house carries trauma, yet the one orchestrating this chaos? Biggs. Ice doesn't even seem to realize how he's being used.

"Well, that's my story, little sis." He laughs, rolling a joint in what feels like 3.5 seconds, then lights it.

"32," he tells me when I ask his age, chuckling. "Met Biggs young. He's been like a big brother ever since — showed me the ropes, made sure I never went hungry. Only family I got in this world. I don't know those people back in the Philippines."

He exhales and passes the joint.

When did I become an avid pot smoker? My tolerance is climbing.

"Are those teeth permanent?" I blurt.

He giggles, shaking his head, sliding the gold pieces off his perfectly aligned pearly whites.

I couldn't believe how gorgeous his teeth were. "James... you're beautiful," I blurted out before I could stop myself.

He blushed, and for the first time, I saw the human side of him. "Thank you, A'maya."

I looked at the joint in my hand, embarrassed. "Nah, I meant... you deserve so much more in life. You're still young, in shape, in Hollywood. You could do anything."

A tense silence settled. "What else could I do, A'maya?" he asked softly.

"Nothing else. Pimping is all he knows, baby!" Biggs interjected from behind. Why does he always creep up like that?

"That's right, my brother! Pimp 'til I die, baby!" Ice said as he got up from the table and high-fived Biggs.

"Breakfast ready, y'all," Biggs announced, his glare still locked on me. Ice walked into the house without a word. Biggs slid into the seat at the table, his eyes still fixated on mine with that damn grin.

"Hey, A'maya, did Maddox talk to you about the new setup?" he asked. I nodded, inhaling the joint Ice had left behind.

"Ok good. Just don't tell the other girls. Our setup is our thing." I nodded again.

He squinted at me. "You know, Chance, you're very valuable, and I like you. Let's draw back on some of those pep talks with everybody. You all positive and shit."

I stared at him. Devilish grin, eyes narrowing.

"What you mean, Biggs?" I asked.

"Nothing, baby," he said, lips ashy, still grinning. "Just don't rock the boat, and it'll be smooth sailing." He winked and left the table.

Was that a threat? And why wouldn't he want me encouraging people to escape his ring? Biggs benefits the most from all of us. At that moment, I decided to start planning my escape—and plant seeds for everyone else to make theirs. I believed I had found my purpose.

CHAPTER 10

Two weeks later, I was sitting on over $82,000. The most money I had ever had at once. Suitcases piled up, and I started shipping clothes home because travel was getting cumbersome. Maddox would disappear for a few days at a time, running off with her reggaeton artist after Biggs flew in his baby mother and a few friends to work for the organization. That's when the vibe began to shift.

Trying to integrate with Biggs' crew proved impossible. Tasha, Biggs' baby mother, was too pretty to belong anywhere near him. At 4'11", caramel-skinned, firecracker energy, and pure ghetto, she ruled her corner of the house. Her right-hand woman was mean, dark-complexioned, and clearly had extensive body work, while another female around my height was slightly pretty but just as ghetto as the rest.

Tasha constantly tried to assert dominance, challenging Maddox and her few allies. Maddox, never one to back down, had a favorite comeback:

"Because you're a boss bitch, and I'm a boss bitch!"

Tension grew unbearable. Biggs tried to move the girls he flew in into a hotel. Sabrina and Baby Doll were clearly missing, so elaborate breakfasts disappeared. Ice ran around, pimping hard. Maddox and I barely spoke since our balcony discussion. A weird emptiness lingered in me. Parties came to a halt while Tasha and her crew were around, which hurt my income—but it gave me more time with Brian.

We went to Dodgers games, Beyoncé concerts, and sightseeing all over California. Each date made Brian more attractive, and my butterflies stronger. I was glad he didn't attend the party—mixing him with this life would have been a disaster. Little did I know, they were already intertwined.

"What you do around here?" Tasha sauntered along the table like a mischievous cat. "I haven't seen you do banks, no mall runs. You just... sit pretty."

I sensed an opportunity to set boundaries without giving her the wrong impression about my relationship with her baby daddy.

"Sis, if you got questions, ask Biggs. Not my place. Way above my pay grade," I said, taking a page from Sabrina's playbook.

"Hmph," she muttered, eyes never leaving mine. She paused, thoughtful, then walked away without a word.

Now I understood why Sabrina had given me that answer weeks ago. Neutrality avoids conflict. I immediately texted Maddox about the encounter. There had to be a reason Sabrina prepped them.

The only problem? Biggs didn't handle things like Maddox, and he clearly didn't respect Tasha.

"Don't question anybody on my team!" I heard Biggs bellow from the table. I stayed seated, scrolling on my phone.

"You're disrespecting me for that white bitch?!" Tasha screamed back.

"I built the platform you're standing on! Now you wanna act brand new!? I know YOU, LEWIS DAVY!"

Their voices collided, rising into a chaotic roar, until all you could hear was Biggs shouting. Something snapped inside me. I bolted for the third floor where they were arguing. The other girls must have felt the same way because we all converged at the entrance at the same time.

Biggs' massive hands were wrapped around Tasha's neck, his eyes burning with something almost satanic. We rushed in, yanking them apart. All I could focus on was Maddox—if she was safe.

"You put your dirty hands on me for the last time!" Tasha shouted, trying to grab things to throw, but her friends restrained her.

Biggs, for the first time without that damn grin, looked remorseful. "Tasha, Tasha baby, I'm sorry," he said, leaning in to grab her arm gently.

Reflexively, Tasha lifted her leg and kicked him in the balls. His natural reaction was devastating: a wrecking-ball right fist slammed into her jaw. Held back by her friends, she dropped like a deflated balloon.

Her two friends started throwing fists, pounding against Biggs' massive frame. He didn't fight back, only blocked, taking the blows like a human shield.

Maddox grabbed my arm. "Ok, we need to leave this shit show ASAP! You got enough saved?"

I hesitated. I'd been spending freely—sending money to my mom, treating Brian on dates—so my stash had taken a hit.

"About 50–60 stacked," I admitted.

"Good. Let's get out before Biggs hits me and tells me the play."

At that moment, Ice walked in through the front door alone. Maddox casually updated him, and he sprinted upstairs to calm the chaos.

We called a black car service and hit Disney World. Maddox looked liberated, laughing through every ride. I, on the other hand, was getting nauseous from sugary drinks and endless twists and turns.

"Ok, Maddox, I'm over this," I groaned, arms full of souvenirs and a Mickey Mouse hat after four hours of chaos.

"Ok. Let's get dinner!" she said while ordering the car.
"Biggs hasn't hit you yet?" I asked, concern creeping into my voice.
"Nope. Not yet," she replied casually, lighting up a cigarette.

We headed to West Hollywood for sushi. Maddox was calmly digging into her dragon roll while I struggled with a green ball of death—wasabi. Sidebar: I'm not a sushi person. I just followed Maddox's lead.
I popped the wasabi in my mouth whole. At first, nothing. Then... vengeance. Fire circled my tongue, burned my throat, eyes watering, water useless. Maddox hung up before witnessing my meltdown.
"You alright?" she teased, glancing at my plate.
"Ha! Don't tell me you ate the wasabi whole! Hahaha!" Her laughter made her eyes tear up, but I could barely focus on anything except the heat.

On the ride back, I carefully circled the topic of our escape in code.
"Did you change your mind about a vacation?" I asked.
"No. I want it more than ever now. I'm thinking Brooklyn with you. Almost five years out here—I've had enough of the West Coast," she said, flicking ash from her cigarette.

"Please, no smoking, ma'am," the West Indian driver said politely.

Maddox took one last pull from the joint, about to toss it out the window.

"No, no, ma'am," the driver pleaded. "We'll get a ticket." He passed her a bottle of water to put it out.

"A ticket for what?" I asked.

"Well, not just a ticket... it could start a wildfire. It's very dry in California right now," he said in a thick accent.

"My bad," Maddox joked.

She turned back to me. "So, what do you think?"

"I think it's a dope idea. And if you still want to work in tech, there's Boston, Philly, Atlanta—people who'd understand you more," I tried to convince her.

"Two weeks. We leave in two weeks," she whispered, leaning close, her scent like success itself. "Biggs will throw more parties so you can stack up. I'll push the girls harder in the banks, and we'll take a few pieces just to shop one last time."

I remembered: "Have you seen a YSL perfume?"

"Mmm," she shook her head, reapplying her lip gloss.

"Ok, sounds like a plan. Don't switch up on me—I'm leaving whether you're coming or not."

CHAPTER 11

The mansion was all black-and-white throughout: white walls, black cabinets, black railings, white steps. The wall to the pool was floor-to-ceiling glass, revealing a jaw-dropping view. Movie theater, sauna, gym—the usual for this zip code. The bathrooms were marble from ceiling to floor, black and white like ink swirling in water.

Biggs and Ice were outside, Ice with a joint, Biggs with a cigar. His damn grin appeared the moment he noticed us.

"Ladies, I owe y'all an apology. Things got out of hand. Maddox, I booked a new crib on my own. There's bad juju here. Pack up—we're leaving first thing in the morning," he said.

"And ladies," he continued, clearly scowling at his baby mother, "this won't happen again. No hoe is gonna play you in my face!"

His grin never left, though his eyes were sharper now. I whispered to Maddox: "I hear you." We both knew what he reallymeant. I'd seen both of them put hands on women—I was questioning our safety.

"Where are those girls? Not scared of revenge?" I asked.

"They ain't gonna do a damn thing!" Biggs shot back. "Tasha and her crew are on a plane home!"

"And Pepsi?" I pressed.

Biggs straightened. "I like you, A'maya, but don't put your nose in my business."

"It's a valid question," Maddox interceded.

Biggs sucked his teeth. "If it makes y'all comfortable, I'll clip her. She's been solid, top earner. Y'all owe me some new girls, so we need another party." That damn grin again.

I nodded and walked to my room, exhausted. Passed out on top of the blanket with clothes still on.

The next morning: breakfast delivered, Brooklyn-style bacon, egg, and cheese sandwiches. Biggs instructed, "Maddox, take A'maya, Ice—Malik will take you to the new crib. We'll meet y'all there."

Malik was cool. Ice? In a weird friend-zone vibe.

The car ride reeked of smoke, like a forest fire. Why did they need their own joint? And never passed it. I didn't know where the house was, even now.

When we arrived, the gothic-inspired door was unlocked. "Hello?" we called. Echo. No answer. Ice flicked on lights; we started exploring.

Elevator in the middle. First floor: massive living room, floor-to-ceiling TV. Second: pool table, bowling lane, paddleball. Third: kitchen, living room, pool outside. On the third floor.

Malik commented, "This place is fresh."

Ice's face said otherwise. "I don't know... gives me a weird vibe."

As we explored, I noticed a slightly open wall in a dark hallway. Ice swung it open: a white door. Slowly, it creaked. Inside: a grey room smelling of dust, rusted metal, leather. A box of keys lay on the floor. A makeshift hallway extended forward, with a bare mattress under a faint red light... then the light shut off.

"Let's get out of here," Malik whispered. We backed away. Ice closed everything up—it was impossible to find again unless you knew it was there.

"No doorknobs anywhere except that trap room," I realized. All doors had push-locks in the ceiling.

Suddenly, someone passed on the second floor. "Hello?" Ice called. Silence. "Spooky," he muttered.

A redhead, like David Cassidy before the haircut, appeared from behind a fence on the third floor. Flushed, nervous. "Hey, guys, you're early. Cleaner didn't get here yet. Whew. Anybody got a cigarette?"

"I don't smoke those," Ice said firmly.

I scanned the furniture—old, decaying, gothic. Dead bees on the windowpane. The man rambled about actors preparing for roles like Johnny Depp and Heath Ledger as Joker.

"The power may go off at night... grid issues," he added nervously.

Ice grabbed his suitcases. "Nah. We're not staying here. Weird, demonic, cult, killer vibes—I'm out."

We left through a garage lined with cameras. Biggs and Maddox pulled up.

"Still got the other house?" Ice asked.

"Yeah, what happened?" Biggs looked confused.

"We ain't staying here—trap doors, spooky stuff," Ice said. Biggs laughed.

Back at the ranch, Maddox and Biggs planned the next party. Tati, Babydoll, and Sabrina arrived—no heads-up for Tati. Pepsi in tow.

The crew hit the banks; Maddox and I stayed behind, wiring money from one account to the next. I watched $375,000 transferred and withdrawn in a single day.

"Damn, Maddy, how much is your cut?"

"About a hundred piece..." she trailed off.

"So, how much before we leave?"

She paused. "I've been saving... almost at my goal." I realized: she was aiming for a few million.

"A'maya, wake up! We gotta go!" Maddox whispered, loud enough to jolt me from sleep. The clock read 2:28 a.m. Midnight dashes had become routine.

The transaction had been reversed, and somehow Maddox found out before it all hit the fan. I grabbed my toiletry bag and the small mouthwash I kept nearby—every precaution mattered. My weekly shipments home were stacked: money orders hidden in clothes, cash tucked deep in boxes. Always staying ahead.

Because of the hour, Biggs had Tati and Malik pick us up—they lived in LA.

When I hopped in the back seat, I did a double take. My YSL perfume, halfway used. Packed in my suitcase. This bottle had been swiped from my room.

"Hey Tati, did you borrow this?" I asked, leaving no room for lies.

Her smoked-out tone, lazy and dismissive: "Oh yeah, I meant to tell you. You dropped it a minute ago. Been using it. Hahaha. I'll replace it next run, sis."

I lost respect instantly. She was young, reckless, and untrustworthy. Dangerous.

New mansion, same routine: explore, find a room, don't get comfortable. Days and nights blurred.

Beverly Crest—just a hop, skip, and jump from the last house. Biggs swore his boys were bringing stars for tonight's party. Justin Bieber, confirmed. I didn't know whether to believe him—sometimes he followed through, sometimes he was full of it.

Ahhh—the aroma alarm clock. Heaven. I followed the scent like a cartoon character chasing a floating pie. The Hutton House was zen perfection: zero-edge pool, fireplace, high-end amenities, sleek wood interiors. Floor-to-ceiling windows on the second floor.

I fell in love with the ambiance. The crew sat at the kitchen island, terrace open behind them. Baby Doll handed me my plate, a warm "Good morning." I returned the greeting and found an open seat.

"Chance, tonight's gonna be epic! Make it a rule—everyone makes it rain on you. Oh shit, let's say it's your birthday!"

Biggs muffled a response with food in his mouth. "I like that idea," he muttered.

Maddox chimed in, refilling her mimosa. "Y'all crazy. But I love the make-it-rain idea. I'll wrap my mind around it."

I prayed over my food and ate, the warmth of this moment feeling like family.

Brian texted, checking in. I kept my word—no mixing business with pleasure.

Ice, mouth full of eggs, teased, "Who got you smiling?"

"You!" I shot back jokingly.

"Not yet" he smiles and chews staring at me.

His Russian girl's face tightened; she looked uncomfortable. "Slow down, pimping," I joked.

I glanced over Maddox's shoulder, she was glued to her tiny computer. Retail sites, percentages flashing next to them: Target 60%, Macy's 65%, Neiman Marcus 70%, GNC 50%. Wait... GNC? Over 50% sometimes? I was up over $100k. Less guilt —I wasn't directly hurting anyone, I told myself.

"Cramps hit. Let's grab something to eat tomorrow," I lied to Brian.

Ice and I kept laughing, sipping champagne, oblivious as everyone else left the table.

"Your girls left you, pimp," I teased, slurring slightly.

"They left to get daddy's money," he shot back, smiling.

I hated that comment turned me on. Drunk, helpless, utterly attracted. I shook my finger at him.

"Toxic man. Stay away from me. I'm going to my quarters for a nap."

I glanced at Ice as I walked away. Mischievous grin. Watching. Waiting.

Everyone was headed out to hustle while Maddox stayed glued to her screens, monitoring everything like a hacker from the Matrix. After an hour of her walking me through the operations, I finally retreated to my room to decompress. Everything had been in fast-forward, and it felt incredible to hit pause.

I stepped out of the shower, wrapped my hair in a towel, and was about to relax when a knock at the door startled me. I assumed it was Maddox, but Ice stood there, the heat in his eyes making the air feel heavy. My heart skipped a beat. "What are you doing here," I said, trying to sound confident.

He smiled softly, loosening his hair from its ponytail as he entered the room and closed the door. "Ice I gotta get dressed" I state boldly but already felt the vibe and knew what was up. "You told me I was beautiful " he said. His presence was magnetic, almost impossible to resist. I could feel the tension between us, thick and unspoken.

We talked quietly, leaning close, stealing glances and brushing shoulders, each word and movement charged with unspoken desire. I had to keep reminding myself—he was dangerous, a force in this world I couldn't fully step into.

Finally, I stepped back. "Ice baby you gotta go," I said firmly. He looked disappointed but respected my boundary, giving me a nod before leaving. My pulse raced long after the door closed, leaving me dizzy with anticipation and the thrill of that closeness. Just when I thought he left Ice reenters the room and walks straight to me.

The tiny towel wrapped around my stacked body stood no chance against these hips you get from mixing Filipino with Black American. My 5'3 coke bottle frame felt small so close next to his chest. My rich chocolate complexioned body that complemented my dark hazel eyes screamed for his. I could feel his passion emitting in my direction. Girl grab ahold of yourself!

I felt between my thighs warm up and began pulsating. He walks in and closes the door behind him. "Ice, I..I..Look I'm not dressed you should leave." I try to convince the both of us. He turns to the dresser, removes his gold teeth and took his hair out of his daily ponytail. "Ok" he whispered as he swooned down on his prey. My mind searched for words they couldn't find. "Ice..." I plead helplessly as one more line of defense.

He picked me up and my natural reaction was to wrap my legs around his waist. We kissed passionately, breathing heavy, he held the back of my neck I held his face by his chin. He put my back up against the wall as we both moaned from all of this built up tension. Ice strong ass in one swoop lifted me up and put my legs on his shoulders. I have NEVER had anyone use their tongue like that on me. My hands gripped the back of his head as I grinned against his face and wall. I let out a shriek when I orgasmed. He carried me to the bed, locked the door put on a XL magnum and walked towards me.

Hold up! When did Asian men start coming built like that! We kissed again passionately as he slowly entered my tight waterfalls and I let out a slight gasp. He took his time and went slow. I lost myself with each stroke he took that got faster but on rhythm.

"I want you to be mine A'maya" he whispered in my ear as he rock my little frame to another orgasm. At this point he could have my social security number and all I own.

I see how he gets them. We fought to switch positions a few times. He got on top and did a finish them move "Whats my name" "James" I said to mess with him. He paused briefly, looked me in the eyes, and laid his body closer on top of mine. "Say it again" he says in my ear with this beastly tone and a stroke he hasn't done yet.

"Say it again he grunt" I bite his ear and whisper "James." He rocked harder for a few strokes, his body stiffened and he let out an animalistic groan. Ice fell like a fall leaf onto my chest.

Stay focused I told myself. You needed some action and he's A PIMP GIRL! Think quick. "Ok get off of me. Now I need another shower before my nap." He looked disappointed. "Damn girl. I don't think no girl ever called me my name when we made love." "Oh we made love huh? I could have swore we just fucked." Ice looked taken aback. I felt power in this moment. I had to keep this wall up. "Come on ice get out. I don't want anyone coming back seeing you leave my room." Ice looking even more shocked got out of the bed and got dressed. He leaned in close to my still naked body for a kiss and I turn away. I wanted that kiss more than water in a desert but he's a pimp. There's no future for us. I locked the door when he left and played with myself before taking a quick shower.

CHAPTER 12

"We got a new game we play here at the pop up parties. You hear your song, I mean if you really hear your jam come make it rain in the DJ!" Maddox announced over the mic holding a drink in the next hand. She had on her best jewelry, small galaxies wrapped around her extremities lighting up as she moved. The crowd roared. Word must have spread around how dope these parties are because more and more people show up. Biggs, of course, figured out how to sell $5000 vip sections with bottles to real ballers. They hired sexy models to come around with drinks and finger food on trays. I dropped song after song at the right part and the crowd loved it each time. I could rock a party with my eyes closed.

I was standing by the equipment but my mind was on Ice. Flashbacks of the "love" we made keep playing in my mind. I can still feel him on me. I still feel his breath on my neck. I searched the room for him to no avail. Snap out of it girl. If you stay focused you can have fun I told myself. A tornado of dollars flying snapped me out of a daze. And oh my God there he is. Ice started throwing stacks of hundreds when I played Crush on you by lil Cease and Lil Kim. He didn't dance or cause a scene. He just cooly stared at me while they sang the hook

But you still don't give me no attention
Listening to what your homegirls mention
Hes a slut/ he's a hoe/ he's a freak
Got different girl everyday of the week
Its cool not trying to put a rush on you
But I gotta let you know that I got a crush on you.

I didn't my best to ignore him and play it cool. I nodded, turned back to the computer and switched the song. Eventually like any good DJ I switched the genre of music to keep the party going. Reggaeton is one of my go to's. Whats the odds as soon as I play one of the biggest songs ever from that genre the actual singer walks in. Yes, he and Maddox play the toxic game together. Maddox the cold being she is stood still and watched him make his way to her. That made her feel important. So many people stopping him to say hello and take a picture but he's fighting to get to her. He approaches the stage and made it rain the entire rest of the song. I damn near wanted to rewind it.
Biggs sat stood on a higher platform watching everyone. His beady eyes plotting on everyone in the room. He makes my skin crawl and I'm waiting on the second Maddox is ready to split.

Biggs wasn't lying. Justin Bieber walked in with an entourage and the crowd went crazy. He came to the mic took a few pictures and shouted couple words to the crowd. There's no stopping Biggs now. He's on a mission to recruit every girl in the party. But I didn't see Ice doing his normal recruitment. You ok? I texted him. "Yeah why?" I don't see you doing your normal 1-2. There was a pause.

"I don't feel comfortable doing that anymore with you watching" he responds. I don't know what to say. This is how he gets his money and I don't want our fling come in between that. He has to understand just as much as I do there cannot be anything more than that. While I find that flattering please don't let me come in between your money. If you gotta pimp you better hop up on the good foot. I texted back. I did not mean that at all but I had to fight it for the both of us. And only God knows if he is even serious. Maybe he's running game and can be trusted as much as we trust Biggs. He didn't respond to my text. Within 20 minuets I see him back in the crowd swimming like a shark through the sea of beautiful women. To see how he made them blush and fall all over him had the opposite effect. I actually was enjoying the view of him run the same game on every girl.

He's so handsome he doesn't even have to work. Even if he tried to make me jealous I could not under any circumstance let it work. I notice baby doll and Sabrina have now joined the recruiting process. Baby doll using tha charm on woman just as pretty as her. Maddox disappeared for the night and I was ready to wind down myself.

As everybody piled out of the house a drunk Biggs sees Pepsi off on the driveway talking to another dancer. He limps over and yells in front of everyone "Don't let me see ya ass around here anymore."

Confused Pepsi asks "Biggs! What did I do?!" As people slow down to watch the show. "My family don't like you so I cant have you around here anymore with ya dusty ass." Embarrassed I saw something switch in her eye. She had enough humiliation from Biggs and Ice.

"You're just upset I wouldn't fuck ya fat ass!" She yelled back. People started to laugh and murmur in the background. Biggs hated being embarrassed. "Keep ya funky ass from around here." He turned his back to walk away. Pepsi spit ins direction as her friend pulled her down the driveway. I watched a woman scorned leave here tonight.

Those boys are reckless on how they have treated woman and one day one of them will be back for their lick back. Or maybe them all.

I took another shower before I went to bed because there was something about a clean body under those 1000 thread count sheets. I walk into the dark bed room, climb in bed and almost yelled. Ice was laying in my bed with his boxers on. “Boy! What are you doing?!” “Nobody saw me come up here I promise.” He pleaded. Ice had taken his gold teeth out. It was like he wanted to leave his alter ego outside. “I’m not having sex with you again.” “Why” “it is too close for comfort. You have girls you have to sleep with for work. What the fuck! No ice! There’s 1000 reasons.” I exclaimed getting more annoyed the more I went on. Not at him. But every obstacle in the way of us even entertaining the thought of being anything. “And this all could be a game to you too! You’re into playing with girls minds and emotions. I do not have time for that.” He looked disappointed the more he listened.

“Look A’maya. Everything you said and more. But for the 1st time in my life I met someone who likes me.” He grabs his chest and continues “ I don't want to pimp you or play with your emotions. Shit. I wanna talk more about how I can change my life and be something else. I avoided you because I was embarrassed, scared, a whole bunch of non pimp ish emotions.”

He laughed. I fought to keep my guard up scared I'll fall for him harder than I have for anyone else. “Yeah aight.” I exhale. “Can we just lay here and talk tonight? Get to know each other more?” He pleads a little. “Ok. Fine. What do you want to know?” “Tell me about everything you remember from day 1”.

I spent the next 2 hours telling him my life story. Ice was a great conversationist. He asks questions, laughed and even remembered names. I was enamored by this side of him. So much more attractive without those ratchet gold teeth. We spoke about careers he can look into and schools he can apply for. He doesn’t have a record which makes finding a job and life change so much easier.

I lay on his chest and we both fall asleep. Im awaken by the aroma of breakfast again and see Ice is fast asleep. I climb on top of him with my body on his and kiss all over his face whispering "Good morning Jimmy. Good morning James.JJ! Wake up." He smiles with his eyes still closed. "Im gonna get you." He jokes and lightly tickles me. I move to the left and feel his manhood poke me on my thigh. Ice began to rub me all over while moaning under his breath. "Let's go eat Jimmy." He giggles and in a voice so deep I felt the bass on my chest. "Let me eat 1st." He flips me over and slides down and puts his head between my thighs. I climax in under a minuet. That boy is a problem. Before I could exhale he slide his body back up and slowly worked himself inside of me. I felt electricity all over my body and fought to control the screams and full submission he desperately wanted. He nibbled on my ear lobe as he ground with each stroke. I was helpless. The only thing I can do now is play tough.

I jumped up when we were done and rushed into the bathroom with a word to turn on the shower. Ice enters the bathroom with an attitude. I got to see him naked with the sun glistening on every muscle. He looked like he was sculpted by God himself. Plus I couldn't believe I was taking all he was giving. Ah hem. "You're going to stop jumping out of bed every time we're done!" He expressed with his eyes squinted and eyebrows down. "Aye look at the pimp. He wanna cuddle. Thats for lovers Ice. And thats not us." And turned and got in the shower.

He followed me in the shower pinned me against the wall and made love to me again. "You wanna play tough? You wanna play tough?" He kept grunting in my ear from behind. We showered together and got dressed. Ice left a few minuets before me so we didn't show up downstairs together.

"Ice," baby doll approaches him with his plate in hand. "The girls thought you weren't here this morning so left for an early date." He nodded as Biggs watched from the corner of his eye taking notes. I made sure to wait a full ten minutes before joining everyone else. The same warm morning greeting from baby doll started my day. Biggs watching me with his eyes squinted.

I purposely don't pay either one of them any mind and start my morning conversation with Maddox. "Chance I got a bunch of Giffy's to swipe today. Wanna get some paper with me today? " she asked between cigarette pulls. I later learned those were gift cards that are somehow broken or loaded electronically. The process wasn't one I wanted to master, just enjoy the ride. "Let's do it." I reply then said Grace before digging into my plate. Ice and I ignored each other completely.

More than usual and nobody at this table is dumb. I tried to be cool and not show I'm panicking on the inside. Oh my God I slept with a pimp. I'm sleeping with a pimp. Oh my God I slept with a pimp unprotected! My mother is going to disown me. This is low i am so ashamed. I look over at him and he's even more perfect than before. I hate him and I hate myself.

"Walmart." She tells the driver and then turns to me "How long yall been sleeping together. A'maya?" I turn red flushed with embarrassment. "It was an accident I was drunk and now I .." lost for words just exhale. "Be careful chance. I didn't bring you out here for all of that. Get your money and stay focused. He's good people's but he's not a good person if you catch my drift." And I totally did. I knew I was in way too deep and his sex is to addicting.

We spent the day hitting up Walmarts and Targets cashing out. Maddox and I had fun making money and buying all type of stuff we didn't need.

We arrived back at the house arms full of bags and buzzed from the drinks at brunch. I guess Biggs and Ice were so preoccupied they didn't hear us come in the huge wooden door. Biggs and Ice were on opposite sides of the room both getting head from last nights party. That's what I get. How could I be so dumb. Yes I knew what he was but I had to idea I was just another act in the freak show. How can I get mad? I told this man this morning we aren't lovers. But damn we just made love this morning. Ice must of felt my eyes watching him and looked u up right as I walked away. And he didn't chase. Didn't say a word. I locked myself in my room and started to cry. What the hell!? He's scum of the earth why am I crying? It's my fault. From the 1st day I met him I knew he was trouble. I hate Maddox for bringing me around him. WHY AM I CRYING!? Out of embarrassment and my feelings being hurt I text Brian.

My emotions had me ignore my better judgement and ask him to pick me up. I took my time changing outfits and made sure to do my makeup extra pretty. Maddox was in the kitchen when I came down with a little over night bag."Ok. I don't need you and Ice little rendezvous to interrupt our flow. Where are you going?" She asks sternly. "Joshua's tree for the night. There's a meteor shower." Ice over hears the conversation and walks in. "A'maya can we talk?" He asks shyly. "Can't right now on my way out." I reply and turn my back to go. Ice follows and grabs me at the door " Where you going with this bag?" He whispers aggressively. "Ice move. Don't you have company?"

Moving trying to get out of the front door. "A'maya you know what I do!" "I do. Enjoy." I tapped him on the shoulder and moved to leave out of the door. The sight on Brian in a black Mercedes AMG enraged Ice. He grabbed me by the arm and flung me around before I could even take a step further. "Who the fuck is that!?"

I could see fire in his eyes. "None of your business. Go check on shorty you had sucking ya dick a little while ago." I reply sarcastically and try to leave. Ices grip got stronger.

" Don't play with me." "You played yourself! Right on the couch!? You couldn't have any decency! Im not mad at you I'm mad at myself and need time away." "With him!?" He asks pointing at the car. I pray Brian stays in the car. "Ice why are you out here worried about me!? You have other females to attend to that make you money." His eyes squinted " I ain't never beg no bitch not to leave me." He snarls. "Good thing I'm not a bitch" I shot back, ripped my arm from his grip and walk away. He stood there like he just lost his puppy. If this is an act to make me believe he really likes me then he should get an academy award.
"Who's that!?" Brian inquires still staring at Ice when I get in the car. "Where we going Brian? I am starving!" Answer a question with a question and you never have to answer.

I'm pretty and I'm from Brooklyn. What the hell is he thinking!? Ice stood in the driveway and watched us pull off until he couldn't see the car anymore. Brian turned up Sade and maneuvered his way down the narrow streets.

CHAPTER 13

The ride to joshua tree took a few hours which we filled with laughter and more in depth conversations. Brian was funny and carefree. He explains how he always wanted to go watch the meteor shower but never had the time or someone to go with. I've never seen a meteor shower or anything in the sky besides an airplane or helicopter in New York City. We both were excited. Maddox texted me on the ride telling me to have fun. I needed a break from the madness that was under that roof. And I needed a break from Ice. Ice. The perfect name because I slipped up. Brian was a breath of fresh air that was gravely needed.

He packed sandwiches and all kind of snacks for our picnic. Brian rented a cabin like container that was very comfortable as we got ready for the evening. It was flat and sandy. Not like a beach but dry mountain and cactus desert. There was a fire in the middle of the encampment surrounded by people staying in nearby tents or just drove up for the celestial show. "Here you go" Brian exhales wrapping a multicolored native looking throw over my shoulders as we sat by the fire. Around 11pm everyone set their sights on the heavens, and she did not disappoint. Balls of light streaked across the sky in every size and color. Every 20 to 30 minuets huge explosions that would be the 4th of July to shame. I fell asleep in Brandon's arms after hours of watching the sky. Brian somehow someway carried me back to our quarters. I enjoyed the fact he didn't drink or smoke so the air was clean and for once in 3 months I have some clarity.

He placed me on the bed and went to get comfortable on the brownish suspect looking love seat. "What you doing" my raspy voice whispered. "I'm gonna sleep on the chair." Mmm hmm. Boy I see your game a mile away. "Come lay with me Brandon. There's lion's and tigers and bears out there." I joke. He giggles while he climbs in the bed with a pillows width between us. If he's waiting for me to make the 1st move he'll die an old man. I'm not the sleep around type of girl and I lose points for this Ice ordeal. I began to nod off when I feel Brandon embrace my body into his. But it didn't feel sexual.

I didn't know how much I needed to be held. I laid there receptive but not making any moves. Nothing. He held me tightly and fell asleep. Nice.

Things started easing up, so Maddox and I quietly shelved our plans for escape. Not because the situation got healthy—just because real life swept us up. California was opening lanes I didn't even know existed. Bookings rolled in: mansion parties, corporate events, and a weekly slot at an exclusive nightclub. Biggs added two new girls with that European, high-cheekbone look. Sweet girls, good energy, quick studies in the hustle.

"I have an idea," Maddox announced one afternoon, lipstick halfway finished. "Let's get dressed to the nines and hit the casino tonight. Ladies—high rollers only. We're not wasting time on small fish."

Classic Maddox: pretty plans, pretty danger.

I was in the mirror, perfecting the last loop of my bun, when a soft knock tapped the door.

"Come in."

And there he was—my addiction in a tailored shirt, buttoning his cufflinks like he stepped out of a glossy poster. He had that silent gravity, the kind that made your breath misbehave.

"Come here, let me help," I murmured, already reaching for his wrist.

"Hey, A'maya."

That voice—low, heavy, familiar enough to rattle me.

I just smiled, nodded.

"Look, we gotta talk."

"About what, Ice?"

"Call me James when it's just us. Please."

The sincerity in his tone dropped something in my stomach.

"Okay, James. Look... we had a moment. A whole space in time that was crazy and perfect and messy. But what do you want from me? This is too toxic."

"I don't love those girls, A'maya." His voice cracked in that frustrated way he hated showing. "I've never felt this way about anybody. I can't stop thinking about you—your morning smile, your laugh, your skin. What am I supposed to do with that?"

Two people yelling about liking each other too much—what kind of curse is that?

"James, we both have to move on. I refuse to let you break my heart. You've never loved before—that means you don't know how. And I'm not about to be your test dummy."

A tear surprised me, sliding down my cheek. He caught it before I could wipe it away.

He pulled me into him, that expensive cologne melting my spine.

"No," I mumbled into his chest, but my body folded anyway.

"Can you teach me?" he whispered into my hair. "Can you help me figure this out? Please?"

Raw. Open. Dangerous.

"I don't know, James. I can try. But I don't like that stunt you pulled in the living room with Biggs. You could've done that anywhere else in the house—right after we didn't use protection? I felt so dirty."

Heat rose back into my chest. The memory burned.

"So dirty you left with somebody else the same day?" he shot back. "Was that revenge sex?"

"You don't know what I did."

"I know you didn't come home. I sat up waiting like a dumbass."

He was deflecting, but I wasn't new to the game.

"Why would you wait up for me? Why would you think I'd want front-row seats to your next circus act?"

He sighed hard. "Biggs has been in my ear saying I'm slipping on my pimping. He set me up. He orchestrated everything. They had just started when you walked in—they were auditioning."

The guilty-little-boy look on his face almost disarmed me.

I didn't let it.

"So was the gun on his lap, or to your head?"

That shut him up fast.

He scrambled for a response, but my phone buzzed—Maddox. We're ready.

"Look, we gotta go." I gave his chest a light tap with the back of my hand, slipping past him. "Have fun tonight."

I didn't look back.

I couldn't.

We were both torn up over each other—sick with it, craving it—but I'd die before showing it first.

The Pechanga Resort Casino was about an hour and a half away in the party bus Biggs rented. Baby Doll, Sabrina, and the other girls danced on the poles while the rest of us tossed dollar bills into the air. By the time we reached the casino doors, the vibe was electric, and everyone was tipsy and hyped.

Maddox and I headed straight for the blackjack table. A few wins, a few losses, and suddenly Ice appeared behind me.

"Let me show you how to win," he said, placing two $100 chips on the table. "You gotta play the double game. Lose $100, next hand play $200. Then $400, $800... keep going until you hit again. That's the only way to get up. Any table, anywhere. Watch."

I had 18, he had 15, the dealer showed 13. "Stay," Ice waved. The dealer flipped a card—a 8. "21," the chubby man yelped. Ice smirked, slapped $400 in chips on the table, drew a 17... the dealer hit 19. Then $800. My stomach flipped. Anxiety crawled up my spine, but I had to watch. The dealer called 21 again after dealing Ice his cards. He had been right. He winked at me, grabbed his chips, and walked away.

Fuck outta here, I thought, rolling my eyes.

I used his logic for the rest of the night, riding a winning streak, when out of the corner of my eye, I saw Pepsi at the roulette table. She was flanked by four tough-looking black guys, all exuding the usual "I got money" aura—chains, watches, bracelets. She was pressed up against the apparent leader of the crew. When I turned to alert Maddox, Pepsi caught my gaze. Maddox didn't have beef with her, so she waved politely.

Pepsi walked over. "Hey, ladies," she said warmly, hugging both of us.

"Hey, P. I'm sorry about how the fellas handled you that night. I wanted to reach out, I just..."

Pepsi cut her off. "I'm not even tripping. I want you to meet the guys I'm with now. They're get-to-the-money type fellas." She smiled like she meant it.

"Aww, thanks, P., but we're all set. Don't need any new plugs right now," Maddox said politely.

Biggs materialized behind her. "Hey, Pepsi. Good to see you," he said, that grin stretching across his face.

"Hey, Big Daddy. I wanted you to meet the high rollers I linked with. Maybe it leads back into y'all's good graces later."

"Ain't no hard feelings," Biggs replied smoothly. "I was drunk that night. My apologies. You and Ice had your thing, and that's my brother—you gotta respect loyalty."

She nodded, but neither Maddox nor I trusted it.

When Pepsi went to retrieve her crew, she made her stance clear. "Biggs, what the hell are you doing?" she spat.

"Playing it cool, baby," he shrugged. "Whoever these guys are, maybe they got some sort of value." That's how Biggs viewed everyone—pawns in his game.

"I don't even want to meet them," Maddox muttered, rolling her eyes.

Biggs' grin made me nauseous as the group approached.

"What's crackin', cuz?" J-Black, the leader said.

Sidebar: That intro was classic West Coast—pure Crip style. I realized we'd been out here four months without any real gang interaction. Out in LA, they're part of the fabric. And surprisingly, they looked like ordinary citizens—no all-blue, no all-red.

Biggs, ever the performer, fluffed up his excitement. "What's good, baby!? They call me Biggs. Heard about you back in Ohio! Oh shit! It's Thee J-Black!"

I didn't know if he was lying to butter these hardened guys up or actually telling the truth. Biggs had a way of knowing and recognizing people everywhere—a superpower of sorts.

"Pepsi told me some good things about y'all's plays," he continued.

"See, that's the problem right there," I muttered under my breath. "Why is she discussing our business with anyone at all?"

I studied J Black's crew—nothing friendly about the dark faces behind dark sunglasses and baseball caps pulled low. Ice must've seen the action too because he made his way over. Instantly, alpha mode kicked in, and another side of him emerged—one I hadn't seen before.

"Hey Biggs, everything alright?" he asked, hand hovering near his hip, eyes locked on J Black's team.

"Yeah, everything's smooth, Ice. This is J Black, Pepsi's people. We were just shooting the breeze. Hey J, what's ya number?" Biggs said, passing his phone to J Black.

"I'll definitely hit you. Let's do lunch or something," J Black replied.

In my head, I knew exactly what Biggs was doing—lining up another plug in case Maddox ever came up short. I'm from the streets; that game was easy to spot. And Ice? He saw it too. Pepsi could not be trusted. Her smug smile barely hid her intentions.

"Definitely. We gotta connect and get a bag. If what she says is correct, sky's the limit. Good meeting y'all," J Black said, licking his lips, nodding, and walking back to the roulette table.

"Nope. Don't like it," Ice muttered, eyes still tracking them as they walked away.

The night felt like an open field for hunters and their prey. Drunk, horny rich men taking a break from their wives, with insatiable appetites. Baby Doll played her role perfectly—the helpless damsel in distress. Tati? She dressed so exquisitely I had to do a double take. The Hawaiian hoe role suited her best, cleavage spilling from a barely-fitting dress, making men think they could have anything they wanted.

Sabrina didn't need a role—she was a natural. A chip slipped into a purse here, a tucked credit card there. Tati would pickpocket the intoxicated men negotiating prices for a good time. She'd pass it to another girl walking by, who'd get it to Maddox at the slot machines. A device in Maddox's bag snatched all the information in under 30 seconds. The girls worked seamlessly, switching roles, returning wallets to their rightful owners.

I had no part to play tonight, so I ordered drinks and sat at the slots next to Maddox.

"What's up with you and Ice?" she asked, slurping on the ice in her drink.

"Nothing," I replied, keeping my tone light.

"Okay... like, I didn't hear y'all getting nasty before? What the hell, A'maya!? Why didn't you tell me? Got Biggs thinking he knows more than me. I don't like being in the dark. We're supposed to be tighter than this."

I let her rant—she was right about all of it.

"And why Ice!? Of all the men in LA, you pick Ice!?" she squealed.

"I actually like him, Maddox. I just hate his lifestyle," I exhaled.

"What ya mother gonna think?" she joked.

"The same your parents would think of your choices, Maddox," I laughed back.

CHAPTER 14

I was already packed and ready by 6:30 a.m. when they came knocking—not that I wasn't expecting the usual dawn dash. I couldn't sleep. My mind wouldn't stop running, and every thought seemed to end on Ice. I hate that name. Shit, I hate James just as much. Could I ever entertain him? No, it's too late; I already know his past. What if we meet later in life? I have to get away from him. Downstairs, Maddox texted. On the ride back to LA, the toll of this lifestyle hit me fully. I hadn't slept properly in months. All I wanted was to lay on a beach with a piña colada and fall asleep. "Maddox, I need a tan and a nap," I thought, whispering it to myself.

"Shiiiiiid. Me too, lil sis. Where y'all wanna go? We did good last night—really good. Let's charter a jet to Cabo!"

Everyone cheered in unison. He looked at Maddox. "Book the trip, baby." Argh. I had never been on a private jet. I climbed the short staircase and fell in love with the cream-colored seats and champagne-colored interior. We played spades and sipped drinks for the under-three-hour flight.

T. he only beaches I'd ever seen were muddy brown, like Jones Beach or some Jersey shore spot. Cabo changed everything. Bright yellow sand, crystal-clear waves slapping the shore, the sun shining hotter than ever, a cool wind caressing my skin—the perfect 83 degrees welcoming me to Mexico. Seven days was already too short.

We stayed at Villa Vegas Dave, the owner's personal residential villa. Eleven bedrooms, each with its own bathroom, furnished with over $2 million in furniture and exquisite artwork. Floor-to-ceiling glass sliding doors opened to views of the marina and the ocean. Maddox and I took full advantage of the short walk to downtown Cabo and the marina.

The private Otis elevator seamlessly transported us between floors, adding a touch of convenience and sophistication.

Ice brought Melinda, his beautiful, dry Russian bottom girl. She kept her distance, likely on his orders. Doll Baby, Sabrina, and Biggs were annoyingly affectionate with each other all week—it became nauseating by the day.

Brian must've missed me because he started texting more often while I was away, asking little by little about my living situation. I'm always at a different location, and he never gets to come hang at my house. I knew it was a mistake a few times letting him cook for me at his place; that led to taking turns at each other's residences. I knew better. I couldn't even lie about being at the last house because he'd stop by.

The pressure made me think—maybe it's time to fall back. That led to the thought that soon I'd have to decide where I really want to be. I don't have to live like this anymore. I've saved enough money to get any apartment I want, anywhere. I've also set up a revenue source outside of their scamming operation. I don't even have to live like this anymore. I have a lot of decisions to make.

The first morning, I thought to myself, "Baby Doll is even cooking in Mexico?" I explored the villa on my way to the kitchen and, to my surprise, there was a butler and a chef. Biggs saw my expression.

"Yea, baby, we do it Big!" he said, followed by that tight-lipped grin. You'd think he'd fix his teeth with all the money he's stealing from people.

This was truly a vacation. We swam, drank, ate, danced, drank, and fell asleep. Maddox and I would lounge by the infinity pool at night, overlooking the ocean, talking about the future—families we wanted, businesses we wanted to start. She was beautiful, articulate, smart. She could do anything. I encouraged her to get out of this lifestyle and manage my career if needed. She smiled, but her eyes often got distant when we spoke of the future.

Biggs ordered car service and we toured the town, hitting every restaurant and club we could find. Seven days weren't enough—especially when there wasn't a dull moment.

On the last day, I stayed outside by the pool to finish my tan. The butler brought over a fruit platter while music blasted from a portable speaker. Ice came outside in shorts, his body glistening with moisturizer, sun bouncing off his biceps and triceps. His hair flowed freely outside of its usual slicked-back ponytail, and he smiled, flashing his gold teeth.

Ice rolled a blunt and sat with Melinda at the edge of the pool. The sight of them together irked me. I hated her and every girl who encouraged this lifestyle. I hated that they didn't have the backbone to refuse being pimped. And I hated that I was blaming them. I was a mess. Of all times for him to come bother me, he chose now. Argh!

"Hey, shawty," that deep southern drawl tickled my ear.

Without looking up from my toenails—I was painting them white, poolside in a white bikini and dark Versace glasses—I said, "Hey Ice."

Silence.

"The weather's really nice out here, huh? You see that view?" He was fishing for conversation. I couldn't help but laugh.

"What?"

"Not the smooth-talking pimp asking about the weather!"

"Stop calling me that!" he shot back angrily.

"What?" I genuinely asked.

"Your occupation?"

"That's what I do, not who I am! And I've never been that way with you!"

"Except when you fuck me RAW in the shower, then have another girl give you head by the evening. Your homeboy forced you into it."

I laughed, dramatically stroking the brush across my big toe. "Weak ass," I whispered.

That ignited a fire inside him. Rage built on his face as he inhaled and exhaled rapidly.

"Bitch! Ain't shit weak about me. I..."

Before he could finish, I leapt out of my chair like a lion attacking its prey.

"Bitch!? Who are you calling a bitch?!" I yelled, throwing punches I learned back in the gritty streets of Brooklyn. Ice blocked each one, trying to restrain me.

"Chill out! My bad! I didn't mean to call you a bitch," he pleaded.

"No! You think I'm one of those girls!" I yelled, trying to hit him, but he kept blocking.

"What girls, bitch?" Melinda screamed from the other side of the pool.

"Mind your business before we jump your ass!" Maddox yelled, entering the backyard from the kitchen, followed by Baby Doll and Sabrina.

I turned my attention to the Russian woman, who subconsciously knew the man she was in love with was in love with me. In that moment, I ran straight at her like a running back to the goal line.

"Biiiiiitch!" I yelled as I threw the first punch. She tried to fight back, but I was faster and stronger. Baby Doll and Sabrina genuinely tried to break us up, but Maddox stood between us, throwing a few hits at Melinda herself. Ice and Biggs finally broke up the fight.

Still enraged, I turned to Ice.

"I swear to God, stay away from me! No more of your good mornings!" I inhaled and exhaled, my voice raw, veins bulging in my neck. "Stop knocking on my door! Stop coming up behind me in the casino! I hate you! Get off me!"

"You go to her room?" Melinda asked in her thick Russian accent.

"You don't question me!" Ice's voice echoed against the stucco walls.

I cried as I walked back to my room. WHY AM I CRYING!?

As expected, the flight was silent. Tati tried to lighten the mood, but nobody was receptive. Biggs lay back quietly for once, a sombrero pulled over his face.

Baby Doll sprawled across his lap while Sabrina rested on his arm—too short to reach his shoulder. Ice and Melinda sat closest to the door, while Maddox and the rest of us were in the back. Even though the flight was quiet, I appreciated that no alcohol was consumed. For once.

I needed to escape. The vacation had been a break from the everyday hustle, but I couldn't stay. California.

Him.

I couldn't even tell if I was homesick or if the veneer of glamour had finally faded. The mansions started to resemble each other—same amenities, mirrored luxury, just designed differently. The parties lost their thrill.

The city had lost its magic.

"Maddox, I'm headed to Brooklyn for a few days.

Doctor's appointments and shit. Next month is Thanksgiving, so maybe I stay until then," I said.

Maddox squinted her eyes. "No, because then there's Christmas and New Year's. I know for a fact you wouldn't fly back and spend those holidays here." She had a point—I hadn't thought that far ahead.

"Maddox…" I began.

"NO!" she interrupted. "You're leaving me!"

"Why are you acting like you've got a warrant out there? Bring your ass with me," I suggested.

Maddox paused. "I can't, A'maya," she trailed off.

"Why not? Come back home! Your parents would love to see you. Come back to the city with me!"

"I can't leave for two months. I have so much work to do. I'm important to this organization."

"In order for it to be an organization, it has to be organized," I said. "That fat old con artist is gaming everybody here. Biggs acts like he's the king on the chessboard. You may be the valuable queen, but he's the most important piece on the board, sis. I've been watching the last 4–5 months. When I tell you, he uses everybody—leverage against each other, or for his own benefit."

She listened intently as I continued. "He doesn't like that I encourage people to do better and remind you this isn't the end-all-be-all. He's actually told me to scale it back. I just need a break from it all—and so do you. No place is home. No place is safe. No stability. I love California like I love a person—but something is calling me back home."

We sat in silence for a few minutes.

"Ok, I'll go. I'll tell Biggs. But follow my lead on this one," she whispered as she exited my room. We hadn't set an exact date yet, but one thing I'd learned here is always: be ready.

CHAPTER 15

You've been avoiding me. Did I do something wrong? Brian's text pinged early Sunday morning. It had been two weeks since we returned from Cabo—and he was right. I had been avoiding him like the plague.

Good morning, Mr. Sir, I typed, referencing our inside joke. Brian's preppy, thoughtful persona had earned him the nickname on one of our many dates.

Would it be bad to say, I miss you?

He replied quickly, **I miss you too**. I felt butterflies stir in my stomach. Ice and I hadn't communicated since our blow-up, and honestly, I was beginning to feel lonely. Maddox was off somewhere, spending the weekend with her Reggaeton superstar—who, as we later learned, was married—on some erotic rendezvous. I was fine with the other girls in the house, but without Maddox, it felt empty. These were her people, at the end of the day.

So, what do you want to get into? I typed. Brian had always been thoughtful, creative—dates with him weren't just outings; they were experiences.

I took an Uber to meet him by the Santa Monica Pier. The weather made it a perfect day in Southern California. I'll never get used to palm trees lining every street, though the distant mountains reminded me nature still had some boundaries here. In L.A., it could be 78 degrees near the coast, but a 30–40 minute drive inland would easily push it to 87. California was visually intoxicating.

We ate on the deck at The Water Grill, right across from the ocean, and had a marvelous time. Brian could keep you entertained for hours, telling jokes and funny stories from his past. The more we hung out, the more attractive he became to me. After lunch, we strolled the pier, got ice cream, rode the Ferris wheel, and he won me a few prizes at the shooting games. He didn't drink much but grabbed a bottle of Prosecco, two wine glasses, took my hand, and led me to the beach.

Sitting in the sand, watching the sunset, sipping wine, laughing together—I hadn't laughed that hard in god knows how long. I spilled my wine reaching for my phone and somehow ended up just an inch from Brian's face. We stared into each other's eyes, and he leaned in for a kiss. Unlike the fiery, untamed passion I'd known with someone else, this was deliberate, careful, like an artist exploring his subject.

I didn't want to admit this next part because I feared judgment. Yes, you reading this—don't label me.

I had made the mistake of sleeping with someone whose career and lifestyle were toxic. He had invaded my thoughts, my body, my system. I tried hating Ice to break his spell, but it was useless. I tried hating myself, and that only led to tears. Going home with Brian was a way to see where my heart really leaned, to step away from that mess. They say the fastest way to get over someone is to get under someone—and it had been weeks since I'd been with anyone else.

I remember the subtle scent of wine, his cologne, the softness of his skin as he guided us through foreplay before tenderly making love. He held my hand and locked his fingers into mine. Brian never took his eyes off of my eyes, searching for his climax while making sure I felt seen, desired, beautiful. He kissed me slowly, with reverence, switching positions until the first light of sunrise.

I awoke to breakfast in bed and the sight of Brian smiling in boxers and a tank top. I had been tipsy when we arrived, but the intimacy of the night lingered. He wasn't scrawny like I'd imagined—slim but chiseled in all the right places.

"Good morning, beautiful," he said, affection in his eyes.

"Oh, now I'm beautiful after you tried to get me sprung! Good morning, and thank you, Mr. Sir," I joked, sitting up to accept the tray with store-bought waffles, bacon, dry scrambled eggs, and coffee. At least he tried, I thought.

"Nah, cut it out. I've been telling you how gorgeous you are since the flight," he replied, walking off briefly, then returning with a fresh tray and turning on the TV.

"A'maya, why do you move so much?" he asked, crunching crispy bacon while scrolling for something to watch.

I had to answer honestly without making it suspicious. "I told you about my friend I came out here to meet. She's a socialite and influencer. She gets paid to stay in mansions, post them, and help blow them up..."

"So she has a partnership or some kind of deal. Me coming out here only sweetens it with my audience," I said, watching his reaction carefully.

Brian nodded, chewing. "Hmm. That's dope. Seems like it could get weary though."

I felt a pinch of irritation but held it in, wanting to see where he was going.

"I guess. I've never seen this type of luxury before. I'm taking advantage while I can."

"Then what?" he asked, halfway through his waffle.

"I'm trying to figure that out. I'm weighing going back home for a few months, see where I really want to be. Constant moving is exhausting. I wasn't thinking about relocating when I came to visit." Everything I said was true—just not the whole truth.

"Well..." he paused, softening. "Until you figure it out, I dunno... maybe you can stay here?"

Ahhh. That's what he was working toward.

"Because I'm barely home anyway," he continued. "I work so much. You wouldn't have to pack constantly. Get a little stability. I promise I'll be out your way."

"That's sweet of you, Mr. Sir. Real sweet." I rubbed his cheek playfully. "But my momma would kill me if she knew I was shacked up with a man I'm not married to."

He smiled—then ruined it. "Then who was that guy who hemmed you up that day I came to get you?"

Think fast, A'maya.

"Damn, Brian. What's with all the questions?" I fake-laughed. "I don't even know what you do for a living. Tell me you're not a cop or something."

He held up his hands. "Okay, okay. You're right. My bad. I just... I got ahead of myself." His voice softened. "I have feelings for you. Real ones. I'm hoping when you decide whether to stay or go, I'm at least part of your reason to stay."

We spent the rest of the day wrapped up in each other. I forgot about everything—my phone, social media, the house, the tension back in the Hills. Brian's apartment had LED lights tucked in every corner, a giant TV that swallowed half the wall, floating shelves stacked with gaming systems, and enough plug-ins to scent a mansion. For a bachelor pad, it was immaculate.

Hours slipped past like water.

When I finally checked my phone—still on Do Not Disturb—I had nearly twenty missed calls and a flood of texts. My stomach dropped as soon as I saw Maddox's name.

Ice was in a real bad car accident please call me!

My entire body went cold.

I jumped out of bed so fast I nearly fell.

"I have to go, Brian. One of my friends was in a serious accident."

He stood immediately. "Let me drive you to the hospital."

We threw on clothes, and he sped across town like he grew up inside a street race. I barely heard him, barely saw him—my mind tunneled into one thought: Ice. Ice. Ice.

How bad?

Was he alive?

Was he conscious?

Was he asking for me?

Brian reached the ER drop-off and gripped my hand. "Call me when you know more. Everything's going to be fine. It has to be."

"Thank you," I whispered, voice trembling. Tears blurred everything except the hospital doors.

The man I loved was somewhere upstairs.

And nothing—not pride, not fear, not the mess between us—was going to stop me from getting to him.

Biggs, Tati, Malik, Sabrina, Baby Doll, Malinda, and Maddox were already in the waiting room when I arrived. Tears, worry, or both sat heavy on every face. Malik explained what happened through shaking breaths: he and Ice had just left the strip club, stopped at a light, when a drunk driver came flying full-speed and plowed straight into the passenger side. Ice's head snapped into the dashboard, and the firefighters had to use the jaws of life to pull him out.

Now he was upstairs—unconscious, battered, barely hanging on. Broken femur, shattered leg, cracked ribs, cuts everywhere. His face was swollen and bruised from shattered glass. When the nurse asked who I was to "James," I didn't hesitate. "His girlfriend."

She led me into his room, and seeing him hooked up to all those machines, quiet and pale and still, ripped something open inside me. The fear, the guilt, the truth. I stayed with him around the clock—reading to him, praying over him, wiping his face, holding his hand even when I knew he couldn't hold mine back.

Two weeks later, he finally opened his eyes. I had fallen asleep in the chair beside his bed when I heard it, low and rough:

"A'maya."

I shot up so fast I almost tripped. I covered his face in kisses, my tears mixing with his dry, cracked skin. "I'm so happy you're alive, James... Jimmy... JJ... Junior," I teased, trying to distract myself from my own shaking.

"Here you go," he groaned, adjusting his body. He didn't remember the accident, so I told him everything, gently, piece by piece. He nodded slowly, processing it. Then:

"Yeah... I remember. And you didn't come home the night before."

I froze. I didn't want to do this. Not now. Not while machines were breathing before he fully could.

"I'm just glad you're awake," I said. "I've been here for days. I need to shower. Here's your phone—everybody's been calling like crazy. I'll come back once I clean up."

"A'maya... please don't leave me."

His voice cracked just enough to betray the pride he was holding onto by a thread.

My heart tripped over itself. Even like this—cut up, stitched up, barely able to move—he still had a grip on me.

"Baby, let me go get dressed. I'll be right back with whatever the doctor says you can eat."

"So you really stayed here with me? Like somebody who cares. Or loves me. Something crazy like that."

The room went quiet.

"Yes, James. I love you. Something crazy like that."

My voice was steady even though my insides weren't.

"And I hate the both of us for it. So get some rest."

I slipped out before he could say anything else.

WHAT THE HELL, A'MAYA?

I couldn't hold it in anymore. I had to tell him. I almost lost him forever.

And saying "I love you" doesn't mean we have to end up together... right? There's different kinds of love. I love my mama, but I also love expensive cars—that doesn't mean I'm marrying a Bentley.

Shut up, A'maya. Yes it does. And yes you are in love.

Ice was finally discharged a few days after waking up, and he rented an Airbnb. He was in no condition to constantly pack up and move at a moment's notice. Crutches under his arms, bruised and battered, he needed help with even the simplest tasks. I stayed with him the first few days—cooking, cleaning, pampering—before the inevitable conversation. Maddox and I had decided to go home for the holidays, which were fast approaching.

I prolonged my departure to make sure he was stable, but now it was time to leave. Ice's face fell. "So... what am I supposed to do? Who am I supposed to spend the holidays with? This is a fucked up time to be leaving!" His voice cracked, laced with frustration and pain.

"I was supposed to leave a long time ago," I said softly. "Before your accident. I need a break from everything."

"Even me?"

"Especially you. I don't understand why you're working so hard to make me fall for you... just so you can get hurt. Call me Jay," I added, trying to lighten the weight in the room.

"I do not want to break your heart. What do you want me to do to prove it?"

"Jay... I'm going home for the holidays. You have all your girls to take care of you."

"You told me you love me," he said, pain and disbelief in his voice.

"I also said I hate that I do. That doesn't mean we should be together. I can't control how I feel, but I can control what I do."

Disappointment washed over his face, his jaw tight, eyes glistening.

"A'maya, why do you act like I don't have feelings? Why do you keep treating me like this?" he vented, raw and unfiltered.

"Jay, I'll stop by before I leave town and make sure you're okay. I gotta go," I replied, gathering my things.

"I love you too," he blurted, voice trembling. "There, I said it. A'maya... I don't know when or how, but we're going to be together."

My chest swelled, my heart melting, but I knew better. It couldn't be true—not now, not ever. I smiled through my tears and began softly singing Erykah Badu:

I guess I'll see you next lifetime...

May-be -we'll-be- butter-flies...

He sat on the couch in silence, watching me go, holding onto hope I couldn't give him.

CHAPTER 16

The next day, I had two suitcases ready for our early morning flight. The house was quiet, the girls out working. Biggs returned with In-N-Out burgers and fries for everyone. We gathered around the table, the clatter of wrappers and fries filling the air.

Maddox blurted it out between bites: "Biggs, A'maya and I are headed to New York for Thanksgiving tomorrow. I'm going to spend Hanukkah with my family, then I'll be back."

Biggs leaned back, thinking carefully before responding. "That's the busiest time of year. Holidays are when the most money's moving. Don't leave me too long."

"I won't," Maddox reassured him.

"I hope A'maya didn't convince you to abandon me," Biggs said, eyes flicking toward me as he bit into his burger.

"Biggs, cut it out. We're making too much money together," Maddox shot back, rolling her eyes.

"I'm going to miss y'all," Tati muttered, mouth full of fries. Baby Doll and Sabrina echoed the sentiment, fries and Sprite in hand.

Maddox booked us non-stop, first-class tickets. We didn't touch the alcohol—just nibbled on snacks and sipped soft drinks. I was anxious about finally returning home. I missed the fast pace, the energy, the pulse of the Big Apple.

We talked about what we would do once we got back. I had always dreamed of opening my own lounge, and I suggested we be partners. She lit up at the idea, and we even made a hypothetical escape plan if things ever went south. Maddox joked about fleeing to France, Switzerland, Ecuador, or Saint Kitt—countries without extradition treaties with the U.S.—promising to text me the flag wherever she landed. The thought made my chest tighten, so I quickly changed the subject.

"How do you feel going home?" I asked. After almost five years, Maddox didn't know what to expect. Her parents were ecstatic—they had begged her for years to come back. What they didn't know was that the girl returning was not the same girl who left.

"If you like it," I continued, "would you consider staying?" I couldn't trust Biggs; he was only out for himself. Maddox nodded thoughtfully, agreeing to take it into consideration.

We laughed about her bizarre fling with the reggaeton star—how Spanish men were so passionate, especially with giving head. Then she wanted all the details about me and Ice, every sexual encounter. I told her about Brian, too.

"My, my, my... you've been a busy little bee, miss A'maya," Maddox teased, hands on her chest, eyes wide in mock shock.

Brian was better for me on paper, but my heart wasn't in it the way it was for Jay—JJ—James—Ice, whatever name he wanted to use. My mind kept circling back to him, and that was the worst part.

"Honestly," I said softly, exhaling, "I just want to leave them both behind."

The words left a weight in the air, and I let myself drift into a nap for the last two hours of the five-and-a-half-hour flight from LAX to JFK.

When we landed, Maddox had arranged car service—a short, stout Hispanic man holding a GOLDSTEIN sign at baggage claim, his belly jutting out over his belt. The city felt like an old lover—familiar, but subtly changed by time and distance.

"Can you drop me off first and come in to say hello to my parents?" she asked, nerves in her voice. "I don't want to go in alone. I haven't seen them in forever."

"Of course, girl," I replied, trying to mask my own guilt. I hadn't seen her parents since she left for California.

The brownstone on Eastern Parkway and Kingston Avenue in Crown Heights looked exactly how I remembered. This neighborhood, predominantly Jewish with a mix of West Indian and Caribbean culture, was alive and vibrant.

On Saturdays, Orthodox Jews walked to synagogue as Jamaican music thumped through the streets and the aroma of jerk seasoning dominated the air. Brooklyn hadn't changed, but I had.

I really missed home.

Her mom greeted us right on the steps, practically vibrating with joy at the sight of her only daughter. Mrs. Goldstein still had that same glamorous, old-school look—pearls, a dark orange haircut curled like Edna from The Facts of Life, bright red lipstick, a loud silk blouse, dark dress pants, and short pumps clicking like she was late for a luncheon.

She pulled Maddox in first, squeezing her like she wanted to confirm she was real. Then she wrapped me up too, smelling exactly like White Diamonds or the knockoff twin of it. High-end urine—that's the only way I know how to describe that scent.

"Girls, come in!" she practically sang as she broke the hug. "Richard, the girls are here!" She grabbed Maddox's smallest bag and hustled up the stairs like she was thirty years younger. The driver grabbed the rest and we followed inside.

The Goldstein house looked just as luxurious as the places we'd been staying—priceless art everywhere, pieces Mr. Goldstein snagged from Sotheby's without blinking. Sometimes I wondered why Maddox chose the life she did when she came from a home like this.

Mr. Goldstein appeared at the top of the staircase with his full head of grey hair matching his short beard and mustache. He wore a yamaka—either for faith or to cover a bald spot, I still couldn't tell. With his black-rimmed reading glasses and that ever-present pipe, he looked like the star of a documentary about brilliant old men with secrets.

"My darling Maddox! And what a treat—hello, A'maya! Will you be joining us for dinner? It's so good to see you girls!" His voice carried warmth like a thick blanket.

"Not tonight, Mr. G, but we're here now..."

"Hopefully for good!" Mrs. Goldstein cut in sharply from the stairs.

"Hopefully..." I said, smiling. "But I'll come back to hang soon. Gotta go see my mom. Maybe I can stop by for Thanksgiving too. I've missed your brisket and babka. Mmm! Please tell me that's on the menu this year."

"I'll make it just for you, A'maya." Mrs. Goldstein cupped my cheek with that soft, motherly hand and gave me a look that made my chest tighten with guilt.

We exchanged our love-you's and be-careful's, and I slipped back to the waiting truck.

The ten-minute ride across Union Street hit me right in the chest. Five months away felt like five years. I missed this concrete jungle—the chaotic rhythm of cars honking like they were talking to each other, the endless motion of people who didn't know how to walk slow.

Outside my building looked exactly the same as the day I left. The old men were still playing chess on the concrete board, talking trash like they got paid for it. Couples passed by, people walked their dogs, and the whole block hummed with the weird, mixed-up energy gentrification brought in ever since they built Barclays.

Some of the younger guys from the building spotted me and rushed over.

"Let me get that for you, A'maya!" Little Keith said, grabbing one of my bags.

Tommy swiped his magnet key to get the heavy steel door open, the one with the scratched bulletproof window.

The moment the elevator opened, the scent of piss hit me like a welcome-home banner. Yup. Brooklyn.

Inside my mom's apartment felt warm. Not just the temperature—everything. Safe. Familiar. Like the walls knew me. The stove was working overtime, the air full of whatever Dominican magic my mother was cooking up.

"Hey, ma!" I called out, dragging my bags inside.

"Mija!" She ran out of her room still in her light blue, flower-patterned nightgown, hair undone, eyes shining. She grabbed me and hugged me so tight my ribs creaked.

"I'm so happy to see you! Tell me everything about your trip! Are you hungry? Did you eat on the plane? Go lie down, you must be so tired from all that traveling—Dios mío, look at these bags!"

She was already pushing one of my suitcases toward my room before I could answer. Her voice flew a mile a minute, filling every corner of the apartment like she never wanted silence to touch me.

Home.

I didn't know how much I needed it until I felt it again.

The apartment had gotten even smaller from all the boxes I'd been sending home—high fashion, stacks of cash, little luxuries I didn't even realize I was hoarding. My mom let me unpack, which took way longer than expected. I opened my closet and stared in awe. I'd never had so many expensive things at once, all neatly organized in one place. Four garbage bags went to Goodwill, and I left a few things behind that my mom loved.

Counting my cash, money orders, bank account, and the crypto Maddox had been teaching me about, I realized I had $380,643.94 at my fingertips. My mind was blown. At some point, I'd stopped counting and just sent the majority home, keeping only petty cash in my account. When had I ever had to pay for anything myself? Food? Nope. Clothes? Nope. Rides? Shelter? Nope. Not a bad deal at all.

By the time I was done, I ate a good home-cooked meal and passed out on the couch watching reruns of Unsolved Mysteries.

SMOOCH! SMOOCH! SMOOOOOOCH!

Wet kisses woke me. "My sister!" Amari, my fraternal twin, was smothering me with affection. I hadn't seen him in almost a year—Yale in Connecticut made that two-hour trip rough without a car.

"Looking good, brother!" I said.

He grinned. "Yea, I sometimes wonder... are you really pretty, or am I vain for thinking you're gorgeous just because you look exactly like me?"

"Shut up, silly!" I tickled him, and the room erupted with laughter. On the stove, queso frito sizzled, golden and crispy, as my mom hummed Celia Cruz.

"I heard you were in California, Miss Big DJ! Rocking for celebrities and making bank! Ok, sister!" Amari nudged me playfully.

"So my mom brags about me behind my back?" I asked, amused.

"Yea, I was out there with Maddox, and we—"

"Maddox?" His expression shifted, a familiar tension surfacing. "Wow. How's she doing?"

I paused. "Brother... wanna smoke a joint with me?"

"What? You know I don't smoke! And when did you start? Damn, that Cali ganja is really irresistible, huh?" he joked.

"I bought a little back with me. I need someone to talk to about this wild trip I just took."

"Ok, let's do it," he said with a mischievous grin.

We headed to the rooftop, the city sprawling beneath us, and I rolled the joint. I poured everything out—Cabo, the beaches, the parties, Ice, Brian... almost everything. I skipped the scamming part; some things even I wasn't ready to revisit.

"Damn, sis, that's heavy," he said after a long drag. "I've slept with some questionable women myself, but I never caught feelings. He must've put it on you hard."

"They've both texted nonstop since I got here yesterday," I admitted, taking another hit.

"Well, if you stay home, let's see who really has feelings and comes to you," Amari replied, wise beyond his teasing.

He pressured me into setting up a night out with him, Maddox, and me. A third wheel? Fine, as long as his friends were fun.

Maddox seemed curious about seeing Amari. She'd always carried a bit of guilt about how things ended with him. Two weeks in New York, and we were already OUTSIDE—hitting 1 OAK, Red Rooster in Harlem, Starlets in Queens, even River Palm in Edgewater, NJ.

CHAPTER 17

Thanksgiving had been a double feast: first with my family, then the Goldsteins. Later, Maddox and I linked up with my brother and his friend Kirk, a med school student, at Lucky Strike on 42nd Street.

Amari and Maddox were inseparable that night, moving as if they were the only two people in the world. I watched them and smiled, realizing some connections just click, no matter how long they've been apart.

She laughed at all of Amari's corny jokes, soaking up every ounce of his exaggerated chivalry. Meanwhile, Kirk was a blank canvas—dry personality, no sense of humor, and completely indecisive. Amari bought drinks for all of us but rarely glanced in Kirk's or my direction, so basically, they managed to have two third wheels on the night.

Back in Brooklyn, Maddox and Amari dropped me off with little explanation of where they were going. I didn't see them again until the next day at lunchtime. Both adults, both doing their thing, and I decided to stay out of it. Soon, they were spending even more time together, with me tagging along like a chaperone or designated driver.

Amari even drove us up to Massachusetts for fried seafood platters, and I lost my mind over full-belly clams. We explored Boston, soaked up city life, and partied in Providence, Rhode Island. Maddox confessed that this was the longest she'd taken a break from work—even longer than after Hasim was murdered. They looked happy, but their relationship was just as hopeless as Ice and I: the doctor and the scammer. Ha! Until she makes her exit, it's all fantasy—a waste of time for both of them.

"Hurt my brother again, and this time I'll hurt you," I warned her, sitting side by side during pedicures.

"Girl, please. He's a player now—I see it all over him. I'll be careful," Maddox replied with a grin. "But give him the same warning. He may be trying to get his lick back. Haha—circle the block and break my heart so we're even." She laughed, just as a second nail technician approached to start her manicure.

Outside, as we were about to get into car service, a man's voice yelled, "Aye Maddox! That you?"

A young, stocky, athletic man with a hazelnut complexion and sparkling jewelry walked toward us.

"Yeah, that's me! What's up, girl?" Maddox exclaimed.

"Budda!" I heard her shout as they embraced. I stood awkwardly to the side. They looked genuinely happy to see each other. I wasn't attracted to him, but his presence gave me the same flutter I felt when I was around Brian.

"Budda, this is my best friend A'maya. A'maya, this is Budda! We ran with each other for a minute," Maddox introduced us. "We got money with each other."

He smiled, nodded, and rubbed his hands together. "You in town for a minute? Let me get your number—I got a play if you're still chasing that dollar." After shaking my hand, they exchanged info for the ride back to her place.

Maddox explained that Budda was connected to a few crews in Brooklyn she used to run plays with back in the day. They did everything from ticket scalping to boosting in malls. Maddox had been the middleman, moving merchandise for them, and she used her school breaks to make extra cash. I had no idea she had been involved with this while we were in boarding school.

She wanted to see what Budda's crew was up to now—always curious about a new play. And here we go again: I want her out of one bad situation, and she's already finding herself in another. I sat quietly, listening to her gush about how much she missed New York, though I knew the real reason for her homesickness was her run-in with Budda.

I couldn't be mad. Sometimes, if you want someone to take a different path, you have to show them the way. And here I was—damn near her employee—still trying to figure out my own next step. I wanted to open my own lounge, but I had no idea where to start.

"Wanna make some money?"

The text came in at 7:43 a.m. on a Saturday morning. What could Maddox possibly be doing the day before Hanukkah? I ignored it, rolled over, and tried to sink back into sleep. Seven minutes later, my phone was ringing.

"Maddox! Argh!" I groaned, answering.

"Can you be dressed by 9?" she asked, sounding like she had been up for hours.

"To go where exactly?" I asked in my raspy, barely awake Darth Vader voice.

"To get the money. Throw on something like a job interview. See you soon," she giggled and hung up. Jesus Christ.

It was an unseasonably warm December morning in New York City. Maddox picked me up in a Ford Explorer she rented for the day. She explained she had been kicking it with Budda all week, and he had shown her another way to make money. They called it "instant credit." She claimed it was easier and less risky than their previous jobs.

The method was simple: open an account in someone else's name at a department store. The store instantly shows the approved balance, and you max it out. If declined, you try again another day with a new profile and employee. Low risk, high reward. "And you don't even have to feel guilty," Maddox insisted. "The person disputes it, the account is refunded, and the store covers it. We're only screwing the banks!"

I knew better, but curiosity tugged at me.

The ride to New Jersey took about an hour. Known for having the most malls per square mile in the U.S., it was perfect for Maddox's demonstration.

Our first stop: Macy's. Maddox used some random person's information and got approved for $12,000. Twelve thousand dollars. We racked up expensive perfumes, designer clothes, and anything high-end we could grab, stuffing it all into the rental.

Next, Neiman Marcus, Zales, Best Buy—even Target approved instant credit that day. At Target, Maddox maxed out $10,000 on gift cards alone: American Express, Delta Airlines, and Visa. By the second mall ten minutes away, I had the swing of things and jumped in, keeping pace with her. The car was packed to the brim, and Maddox had a backpack full of gift cards.

"I'm starving," I confessed, exhausted.

"Well then, River Palm!" she declared, taking the last exit in New Jersey before the George Washington Bridge. The legendary steakhouse in Edgewater was as over-the-top as the day itself. Rockefeller oysters, crab cakes, sushi, filet mignon, and a few lemon drops later, Maddox paid with a couple of today's gift cards.

"So, how does the money work? Same split?" I asked, swaying slightly from the alcohol.

"Nah, today we do 50/50," she slurred. "We split what we made, and I just break Budda off. He'll get rid of the merchandise. If we keep the gift cards, we keep 100% of the value. Cash out? Less. I'm not pressed, so we hold."

She went on, animated, about Budda's crew and all their hustles—from call centers to tax prep to car accident insurance scams. They had systems where we didn't even need fake IDs anymore. Legit accounts would deposit $20,000; they'd take $10–12,000.

Listening to her, I realized something: I was addicted too. I felt guilty for enjoying it, judging it even, but I couldn't deny the rush. Sure, I wasn't planning a career in this lifestyle, but at 28, this was undeniably one of the highlights of my life.

"So do you plan to go back to L.A? It sounds like its easier and more opportunity at home?" I ask making it sound more like a legit job or something other then the organized crime it was. "I really want to. I think I am going to go wrap things up with Biggs in LA, get my things out of storage and come home. It's less pressure out here. Don't get me wrong I love the weather, the luxury and everything in California but nothing feels like New York City." She smiles, switching lanes on the FDR highway headed towards the Brooklyn bridge. I couldn't agree more.

Maddox spent Hanukkah with her parents and even invited me over for a few activities they were doing. Amari tagged along to say hello to her parents and catch up. Mr. Goldstein was thrilled to see my brother and how he's grown. He apologized to Amari for how he wasn't exactly receptive to Maddox and his relationship years ago.

They had shared jokes and old stories in the den as the ladies prepared a few dishes including Matzah ball soup, brisket, fried foods like latkes and donuts. Growing up with a Jewish best friend meant diving into the culture. Since the Goldsteins have always been so loving it was easy to embrace it and learn so much.

"So does this mean you two are getting back together?" Mrs.Goldstein inquires sipping her soup a little annoying louder then I would prefer. Awkward! I looked up surprised with my eyes wide open. "Ma!" Maddox blushes. "Rachel!" Mr. Goldstein shouts. "Whaaat? I just wanted to know. It's good to see Amari. He's looking good, doing good..." she trailed off. Many moons ago they disapproved of my brother dating their daughter but here we are today and her Mrs.Goldstein is trying to marry her off. "Mrs.Goldstein Maddox and I are great friends and I am happy to see her after all these years..." Amari explained as I couldn't help but to notice the disappointment behind the half smile Maddox displayed. "Well I am proud of Amari and all he's accomplishing. Keep up the good work." Mr. Goldstein raise his grape juice in a toasting manner.

"You minds well stay and leave the 26th. Christmas is in ten days. We have been getting money the last two weeks what are you rushing back to Biggs for?" I pleaded with Maddox. "He's has been calling saying he needs me for some big multi million dollar play he has out there. I want you to come with me and get a piece. I promise after this I'm done. Come home and start a family with you brother finally" she jokes. The time away from California, Brian and Ice was what I needed. Brian would text occasionally to ask how I was doing and when was I expecting to come back. Ice stopped responding to my text eventually. He was upset and claimed I abandoned him when he needed me most. Of course being self centered and not understanding was the characteristics of a typical man. Ill just pull up on him when I get back.

“Hello?” Maddox snaps me out of zoning off. “I can not leave my mom alone for Christmas. Amari is leaving the 26th, so I guess ill have to take flight and meet you out there.” I replied.
She thought for a minuet, her face posed in deep thought. “Ok ill stay. Damn it! I dunno. I feel more comfortable when you’re there. Like I don’t feel alone or by myself. I’ll book our tickets tonight for the morning of the 26th A’maya.” I agreed.

CHAPTER 18

I like taking red eye flights first thing in the morning. The waking up during zombie hours and rushing around in the dark, moving fast to catch a flight. Maddox and I didn't pack any bags, just carry ons with underwear and toiletries. What's the point when we are going to accumulate tons of new clothes anyway. On the flight back we took advantage and got super hammered. The flight attendants had to ask us to keep it down a few times when we got too loud joking and laughing. We had to stay in a hotel when we landed because apparently Biggs couldn't book the houses like Maddox. That is the first red flag that stood out to me. He wants to get back into the houses.

Biggs, Tati, and Sabrina greeted us in the bar area of the L'Ermitage Beverly Hills. We hugged and had more drinks by the pool. I expected to see Ice with them but didn't want to ask about him in fear of looking thirsty or too open. Biggs was still doing his annoying closed lip grin as we celebrated life. Maddox and Biggs would whisper as they passed their cell phones to each other in a corner while the rest of us joked around. I didn't get it.

If Maddox was making more money in Brooklyn with Budda and took a bigger percentage what exactly did she need with Biggs. What did he have on her or better yet what was this deal he had worth millions of dollars. I didn't trust it. I had the same disdain for him I had before I left and as a matter of fact it may have grown. I stayed out of their way purposely but had every intention to ask Maddox whats on his mind when we reach our room.

Biggs walks in my direction "I told your boy you back in town and he's on his way on over here." He grins. "Who's that?" I ask knowing damn well he's talking about Ice. "The president of the united states" he jokes and everyone laughs. "You know who the hell I'm talking about. I told him you looking good too.

Gained a couple pounds in the right places when you was on the east coast"
"Shut up. You sound like a creep" I shot back not knowing if I should be flattered or insulted.

A few hours had passed and I was still exhausted from the flight. I bid good evening to the gang and headed to my room.

The office suite had a dark golden wall paper wrapped around a white and nude colored room with a fireplace, couches everywhere. It was a big room with a living room the works but it was just right for me. The beige colored marble bathroom had a vanity and was relaxing as I took a bubble bath in the extra large bathtub. There was a knock at the door as soon as wrapped the bathrobe around my body. "Who" I asked. "Its me A'maya." The sound of the bass filled southern drawl made my heart skip a beat before it melted.

I played it cool and opened the door to let him in. I didn't know it was possible for him to be more beautiful then before. "Hey Ice ice baby." I joked in reference to Vanilla ice's song. "Ha you funny. I missed you. You look good." He came in and hugged me. I felt between my thighs begin to pulsate. No gotdamn it! I cursed my self. He wrapped his arms around me and my body attached to his like a magnet. I fought the feeling not knowing if he can tell I belonged to him. His cologne filled my nostrils and his heart beat echoed in my left ear. His long strong fingers rubbed my back through the thin robe. I was determined to stand my ground. I broke away from his loving grip "I missed you too. How are you feeling? You healed up pretty nice" I ask walking towards the long dining room table in the room to take a seat. "Yeah I'm good. Been working out eating clean staying out of trouble." He smiled without his gold teeth in. He knew that drove me crazy. "How's business" I asked. "Here you go." Ice exhaled. "No I am serious. Ok never mind then umm what else have you been you too?" I searched for a conversation. Ice joined me at the table and we talked about my trip back home. He asked if I saw any old boyfriends. I was amused by the slight jealously. He told me he has been up to regular business but saving up his money and working towards changing his life. My heart wanted to believe him but my mind kept saying this is all game. But if it is what's the point? Why keep chasing me? He doesn't seem like the type.

Just when the conversation was about to get too emotional there was a knock at the door. Maddox twirls in with the energy of a princess. "Hello Ice." She voices in her playful British accent she does from time to time. He stands up "Hey Maddox good to see you. Well Imma let yall get too it. Im staying here too so maybe we can grab something to eat later yall." Ice says before walking out. Maddox waits until the door closes "Uh huh miss I'm so tired good night yall. What was yall up too?" She playfully asks. "Cut it out. You heard Biggs downstairs earlier. Ice just showed up. I don't even know how he found out what room I'm in. Unless you told him!" We both laugh because she's the only one tha knows what room I am in. "Oh yeah I forgot I did earlier. Hahahaha" I was glad she did because I was happy to see him but I was too drained to go anywhere tonight I need a nap.

I started keeping a ledger, jotting down everything from gift cards, cash, and high-ticket items to hotel expenses and tips. Every cent mattered if I was going to make this move. Maddox noticed the change immediately.

"You're acting all responsible all of a sudden," she teased as we rode the elevator down to breakfast in the penthouse suite. "What's up? You finally realized you're not immortal?"

I smiled, though my mind was elsewhere. "No, just thinking ahead. I can't stay in this forever."

She nodded, understanding but not judging. Maddox had a way of letting people chase their own paths while still pulling them along for the ride. "Fair. Just don't slow down too much. The money won't wait."

I glanced at the other girls. They were all buzzing with energy, checking store apps and comparing approvals from the night before. It was exhilarating, chaotic, addictive—and I needed out. I couldn't shake the excitement, but I also couldn't ignore the endgame I had in mind: a lounge of my own, a space that I built and owned, free of the hustle and the constant movement.

That night, while Maddox and the crew planned our route for Phoenix, I stayed behind in the suite, sketching out floor plans, budgeting, and jotting down ideas for menus, décor, and staff. The contrast between the glitzy, fast-money life I was living and the grounded, controlled world I wanted to create was dizzying.

I realized it wasn't just about the money—I wanted freedom. A place where the chaos didn't follow me, where the thrill of survival wasn't my daily routine. I wanted to feel pride in something that was mine, something I could touch, walk into, and say: I did this.

Maddox knocked lightly before entering. "You still here? Everyone's heading to the mansion party."

I looked up from my notes, a small grin forming. "Yeah, give me five. I'm almost done mapping the space."

Her eyes sparkled with amusement. "Mapping your empire, huh?"

"Exactly," I said, standing and stretching. "But the thing is... the empire won't build itself. I have to make sure this isn't just another one of those thrill rides. This time, I want control."

She smirked knowingly. "Good. Because when you do it, I'll be first in line for a reservation."

I laughed. "Deal. But first, we finish this last trip without anyone noticing I'm slowly checking out of the life we've built here."

Maddox nodded. She didn't need to say it, I didn't need to say it. We both knew the game was ending for me, but the thrill? That would always linger in the back of my mind.

And just like that, my exit strategy wasn't just a plan—it was my obsession. Every mile, every hotel, every store became a countdown to freedom.

We got out of the Tahoe, the crisp night air carrying the faint scent of the ocean. Maddox led the way up the winding driveway, her heels clicking against the marble steps. The mansion's lights were blinding, making the palm trees cast giant shadows across the perfectly manicured lawn. Inside, the place was even more insane—white leather couches, floor-to-ceiling windows, chandeliers the size of small cars, and a bar stocked like a private club in Monte Carlo.

Chris Brown himself was in the corner, laughing with a group of people I vaguely recognized from Instagram. Maddox nudged me, whispering, "Try not to look like a deer in headlights. We know these people." I nodded, trying to act casual, though my heart was racing like I had run a mile.

Tati, Baby doll, and Sabrina disappeared into the crowd, effortlessly navigating through entourages, camera flashes, and cliques of models and athletes. Maddox stayed close, making introductions like she was the hostess of the universe. I trailed behind, feeling like a tourist in a world I could barely comprehend.

"Did you see those cars outside?" Maddox said, nodding toward a Ferrari that looked like it had been custom-built for royalty. "That's probably the cheapest ride here."

I laughed nervously. "I think I just overdressed."

"Overdressed is better than invisible," she replied, flashing her signature grin. "Just follow my lead."

Somewhere between a round of tequila shots and hors d'oeuvres I couldn't even name, a group of retired football players walked past. Terrell Owens gave Maddox a nod; she nodded back as if they were old friends. I tried to remember all the names she had mentioned, but it was impossible to keep up. Everything was moving too fast—the music, the chatter, the flashing cameras.

Eventually, Chris Brown came over to greet our group personally. Maddox, Baby doll, and Tati leaned casually against the railing, exchanging pleasantries. Chris eyed me for a second, giving a small smirk, then turned back to Maddox.
"She's with me," Maddox said quickly, linking her arm with mine. "She's new to the scene."
Chris nodded, a half-smile on his face. "Welcome to the madness. Yall coming to my house for the party right? " He demands more then asks.
I laughed, realizing how insane the night had become. From learning construction lingo to navigating celebrity football games and Malibu after parties, it felt like life had fast-forwarded into some hyper-reality I wasn't sure I was ready for. But I couldn't deny it—I was living it. Every chaotic, glamorous, absurd second of it.
Maddox caught my eye across the room, raising her glass. I raised mine back. No matter how wild this world got, somehow, we were still a team. And for tonight, that was enough.

We arrived at Chris's sprawling gated estate. Before you get to party inside the house a huge Caucasian man with even bigger muscles and a beard takes everyones phones and places them in a bin until the festivities are over. Chris's house was beautiful from what I saw as we were ushered into the basement where the guest are allowed. Bow wow, Omarion, and Scrappy entertained the room full of pretty girls that came to the afterparty from the party earlier. I played pool with some guy that was apart of their entourage while we all smoked weed, drank tons of Liqour and partied the night away.

Omarion was doing the dance from the icebox video to impress the ladies. You can imagine my disappointment when the shindig was canceled within a few hours and I didn't even get to meet talk to Chris! I didn't want to be all up in his face at the game, especially knowing we were coming here. Walking to our car I overheard someone saying his girlfriend got upset and they had a argument which prevented him from joining us. What a bummer.

Tati, Maddox, Sabrina and Baby doll remained super drunk as we tried to figure out who was sober enough to drive back. I volunteered to be the designated driver even though I was equally hammered. Malibu was scary movie dark with barely any street lights to illuminate the path. The alcohol somehow placed the double lines at the top of the windshield and part of the ceiling. I drove us back to our rented mansion without setting my eyes down on the actual road.

I noticed Tati wasn't her usual self. As the rest of the loud, drunk girls chattered away she sat in silence. "You good Tati baby?" I asked the little thief. She just nods. "Liar! What's wrong Tati?" Maddox slurs. "Nothing. He just texted me and told me his wife knows about us. He tells me he can't see me anymore!" She starts crying. I dont know who is but I assume it's her guy she's been seeing. "Girl fuck him!" Sabrina yells in support. "A text message? He didn't even have the decency to see you or call you? But a sneaky cowardly text? He doest deserve you!" Baby doll add in. The ride home we console her and try to conjure up ways to get revenge for breaking our friends heart.

CHAPTER 19

We all woke up to hangovers and felt bad making Baby doll cook so going out to eat became enticing. While I stumbled over this room trying to get myself together there was a knock at my bedroom door. "Come in" I chime with my back facing the entrance. "Good morning maganda" Ice's bass filled voice echoed.

I turn around and instantly melt inside but kept a cold exterior. My god is he gorgeous. "Who is Maganda?" I question. He's holding two coffees and passes me one. "Maganda is beautiful in Tagalog. The native language of the Philippines." He smiles then continues "Light and sweet how you like it. Heard you guys had a rockstar night." I take the coffee and lean in for a hug. My head always lands on his perfectly chiseled chest. "Thank you." I moan. He smelled amazing and looked even better. But I, A'maya from Brooklyn will not break. "You're welcome" he voiced, leaned down and kissed my forehead.

At The griddle on Sunset Boulevard, the gang ordered everything on the menu as usual. Malik met up with us and it felt like the old days again. Ice told me the only way to beat a hangover is to drink more liquor. I knew better but threw back mimosa after mimosa with him. We were locked in each other's eyes and paid the rest of the world no mind.

He didn't have any girls with him and I did not ask where they were. I loved having his undivided attention all to myself. The bill came and this time everyone fought over who was going to pay it.

That small gesture knowing everyone had their own money and didn't have to fear a card declining bought a small smile to my face. We came across loud, borderline obnoxious as we exited the restaurant. Ice and I fell behind the group locked in each others eyes telling corny jokes. I didn't even see him approaching.

I turned my head to see a confused Brian standing in front of me. I cleared my throat as I grasped at any thoughts my drunk mind could grab. "Eh hem. Brian this is James. James this is Brian." Neither of them paid me any mind as they began this intense stare off. Ice and Brian saw each other that day and I never gave a clear answer on who either of them were. I could see the expression on Ice's face turn colder by the second. "Yea, that's the muthafucka that picked you up that day." Ice growls. "Brian what are you doing here?" I ask, trying to change the subject as I slowly make my way from under Ice's arm. Without taking his eyes off of Ice he responds "A few of my boys are in town and I was showing them around. This is A'maya fellas." I was embarrassed because I didn't know what he told his friends about me or what we were to each other. I waved to the three casually dressed gentlemen behind him. "Ok let's go."

Ice grabs my hand to lead me away. "Hold up partner. We weren't done talking. You go ahead." Brian jumps in. "What?" Ice coldly quips. "You heard me nigga. Move along." At this moment I do not know why Brian is playing a tough guy but I wasn't certain he could take Ice in a fight.

Was he drunk or showing off for his boys? Ice didn't respond he just swiftly turned his body as his muscles began to expand under his t shirt. I knew he was ready to start some shit in front of all these people on sunset boulevard. I jumped in the middle of them before Ice could take another step while gently rubbing his arm. "Hey Brian. It is so good to see you. I wasn't expecting to run into you. Can I call you later? Hmm?" I ask sweetly using these green eyes to try to get my way. He looks at Ice one more time before relaxing his glare on to me.

I honestly felt bad about this encounter. "Yea. Hit me when you're done with the circus." Shit! Why did he have to say that? All of the testosterone was building up on each side. The next thing I felt was Ice push me out of the way, cock back his arm and swing on Brian. The rock solid fist hit him on the right side of his jaw with the force of god. Brian could take a hit because he stumbled backwards one step then rushed at Ice. They threw blow after blow before I yelled stop it and tried to jump in between them. His boys jumped in to break it up as Biggs and the rest of our team finally runs back over.

They had consumed so many mimosas and wasn't paying attention to us behind them. "Break it up!" The guys yelled separating the two men that were still trying to get last second hits in. "Next time I see you I'm breaking your jaw!" Ice screams and spits in Brian's direction. "Do it now bitch!" Brians yells back licking the small amount of blood from his busted lip.

I wasn't sure if I was mad because I was drunk or because the stunt Brian just pulled.

He could of let it go, I had it under control. "Brian, what the fuck!?" I slurred and pushed him. "What!? Who is he to you!?" He shot back nursing his jaw. I didn't know at that point how to answer. Brian was better for me but my heart belonged to Ice, James, jimmy. I exhaled and walked off.

The ride back to the house Ice and I rode in silence as the rest of the crew was loud and talked amongst themselves. When we pulled up J black was in the driveway with two of his goons. I hated the sight of them. I did not trust him and did not feel comfortable when he was around. Maddox retired her small laptop and they all sat down to have a meeting in the dining room area. They began to plot under chandeliers that cost more money then what I have saved up. I decided to head to my room, take a shower and sleep off this liquor.

As I wrapped the towel around my head I heard a knock at the door. Deja vu. "Yeah" I respond, headed to my suitcase to retrieve a pair of underwear and something to sleep in.

Ice walks in and I finally understood his name. The air shifted in the room when he walked in.

He had a bruise near his forehead area and a small knot to accompany it. I instantly get turned on at the sight of his wounds. I have never had two grown men get jealous and fight over me. I did not know what his angle was so I played cool not to look like the damsel in distress. "You ok baby?" I ask softly, as I place my hand on his face. He gently grabs my arm and looks me in the eyes. "Who is this clown A'maya? You sleep with him?"

He questions. I did not want to lie, for what? He's a damn pimp and probably sleeps with all of his girls daily. I am not going to tell him I only slept with Brian to try to fall out of love with him. To try to feel something for someone else. I am a mess and its all his fault.

"That's Brian. We umm." I couldn't bring myself to say it. "Ya'll fucked!" He inserts abruptly. "Look Ice." I try to reason " You had a lot going on at the time and who am I kidding you probably still do. I walk in you're getting head from some random slut off of the street. We just had unprotected sex. I didn't know what to do." "Thats when it happened!? So you go sleep with somebody the same day!?" He demands. I could see the hurt in his eyes and apart of me wanted him to feel how I felt that day. "You did it first! So pimps are narcissist huh? HA! I am not one of your hookers Ice! And I'm not going to argue with you in a towel. Can you excuse me?" "No! I'm not going anywhere!" He shot back. "You dont notice I haven't bought any girls around? You haven't noticed little changes? No! Cause you too busy with ya head up his ass!" He growls. "Excuse me? First of all im not up anybody's ass! Secondly what you want a cookie? You don't bring your dirt around me so im supposed to be happy?"

I yelled back as I finally realized his efforts. He was right. I did notice they haven't been around but never gave him credit for that. I wasn't aware of him trying to make amends and give me the respect I deserve. But I am a woman and we will argue even if we are wrong. He comes close, lightly grabs me around the neck, leans into my ear and whispers "Yes, thats the point. Keep playing with me. I'll knock out every mutherfucker you bring around." I could feel his manhood harder and rise on my thigh. I smacked his hand away and moved back a few steps. "No you are not! I do what I want to do!" I try to sound assertive as I felt myself began to moisten and throbbing between my legs. He came closer "You think Its a game?" He asserts with passion in his eyes raging like a bonfire. "I am not your girl Ice" I whine. "Yes you are. You are mine A'maya." He deeply whispers, wraps his arms around my waist, pulls me in and begins kissing me deeply. I could not resist him. My brain sent signals to every ligament in my body to pull away, retreat damn it! Nothing. I melted quicker than Mr. Softy on a hot summer day. I couldn't help the moans reacting to every move of his hands. Ice threw me on the bed and ripped my towel off of me midair. He climbed on top of me and kissed me deep but it felt different. This felt like he speaking body language and trying to get his girl back or even convince her to stay. I grabbed the back of his head as I kissed him back in the same language. This time wasn't like all the other times that were intense and filled with passion. This time we made love.

Ice and I came downstairs together doing our normal laughing and joking. Maddox was still at the long, expensive looking table with Biggs, J black and his boys. I greet everyone. "Yea shorty. We having a new years party tonight!" J Black informs me. Confused I look at Maddox. "Yea, I was waiting for you to come downstairs Chance. We think we could make some money tonight. And we have never partied with the 60's!" She expresses trying to sound cool. "Exactly! And say, Biggs you invite them celebrities. We can tax whoever ain't check in. Thats another play I can bring you in on." J Black chimes in. "What you mean playboy" Biggs jokingly inquires. "Aight, so lets say your boy, I don't know, lets say some big shot rapper shows up. One of the homies will press him and act like he's gonna rob him or cause bodily harm. I swoop in, make everything copasetic and now whenever they're in L.A they pay for protection. If they live in Cali well thats a monthly payment! Rappers been checking in since the 90's" J black continues. "So fill the room up with stars and we can get some residual income. Shiiiiit!" He jokes as he and his friends give each other high fives also known as dapping up. J black was correct when it came to checking in. In L.A culture its "to pay a visit to" someone often as a way to show respect, particularly in the context of gangs wanting "blessing" for being in their territory. A less common slang meaning can also be to report your arrival to an authority figure or gang member, to intimidate someone or get their permission to be there.

I hated what we did to get money but I also convinced myself we are beating the system. But what J black is suggesting is outright extortion! How could I intentionally invite any celebrity that I know and send them into a trap. I wasn't going for it and I had to think quick. "Damn, I wish you told me earlier Maddox. Me and Ice planned on watching the fireworks on the boardwalk when the ball drops and I got a gig right after up the street."

I lie in my most convincing voice. But Maddox being my friend, and a expert mind reader, knew it wasn't the truth but also understood why I didn't want to be a part of it. "Damn, he ain't tell me." Biggs states looking at Ice. "We just decided upstairs." Ice responds assertively. Out of every effort he has made to show growth, this moment made me so proud of him. Ice stuck up for himself and didn't back down to Biggs manipulating ways. "Oh aight player. That box got you wrapped up I see." Biggs jokes back as J black and his guys laugh along. "Watch ya fucking mouth, my brother." Ice snarls in a deep, calm, callous voice. "Meant no harm my guy. Ya'll enjoy yourselves tonight. We will find another DJ who isn't as good as you Chance, but I'll try." Biggs sarcastically announced followed by his grin.

Ice and I had no idea about the fireworks or where to find them but eventually we gathered all the information we needed. "Isn't New Years a big night for a pimp?" I genuinely ask on our ride to the Santa Monica pier. He takes a moment "I am right where I need to be." Ice exhales then grabs my hand.

We played games, ate food and watched the fireworks explode in the sky at midnight. Ice grabbed me and kisses me as the loud booms went off and colorful lights danced across the sky. My mom had called me at 9pm because New York's 3 hour difference had her ringing in the new year before me. I let her speak to Ice so he could wish her a happy new year. When Amari texted me happy new year I told him I was with Ice and he cracked a few jokes. Surprisingly Brian texted to wish me a happy new year. Those funny butterflies rose in my stomach as I wished him a happy new year back. I have to make some decisions for this new year and make them quick. I'll start doing more investigation on my lounge, devise an escape from this life and from him. There is no future for me and Ice even if he's hiding his stable of women. Argh! I'm such a mess.

CHAPTER 20

I awoke to the aroma of Baby doll in the kitchen whipping up the first meal of the new year. As I went to stretch my arm bumped into Ice's chest. What the hell? I guess we got in so late I didn't remember him getting into bed with me. He lay asleep with his arm still around my waist. I slid from under his grip and just admired his beauty for a moment. He slowly began to open his eyes. "You finally got what you wanted, huh?" I whisper. Ice stretches and groans "What you mean by that?" "Us sleeping together." I joke and push him. "Nah, you told me to come lay with you.

We came home last night, I walked you to the bedroom door and you asked me to hold you." He responds as he sits up under the sheets. I scanned my mind for the last memories from last night and it was true. It wasn't out of lust, but true companionship. "Hmm. I must of been drunk." I respond cheekily. He voices "yea aight" as he grabs me to pull me in and tickle me. "You want to eat in bed?" I ask as he types away in his cell phone. Ice's face was focused on whatever he was doing. "No my cherie. I gotta get out of here and do a few things." Ice hopped out of bed and put on his clothes from last night. He kissed me on the forehead and headed towards the door. "Thats all I get?" I ask expecting a kiss on the lips. "Neither of us brushed our teeth yet and I'm a smoker. Instead of stuffing a whole bunch of gum in my mouth I'll just see you when I freshen up." Damn I love this man.

Ice had enjoyed those couple of weeks he had to himself in the home he rented while he was on crutches. He decided to work something out with the owner and stay in the property longer. Maliak is Ice's right hand man when it comes to anything in life. He decided to bring him in to help with his operation with the girls. Ice rented a separate apartment for his girls and didn't stay under the same roof with them anymore. He began saving his money up to do different things with his life. Maliak was surprisingly good at the pimp trade and recruited three new girls which bought the total to six including Ice's main girl Malinda.

They weren't your hat with a feather in it, loudly dressed, girls on the corner, type of pimps. They had rich cliental and high priced call girls. Malinda was a very sought after woman and was Ice's crown jewel. She was the madam of the house and taught the girls everything they needed to know from posture to how to carry yourself around powerful men. Ice would get a card or "swippy" as they called it to take his girls shopping giving the illusion he is spending his own money. I finally figured out why he paid that bill months ago and why he would always pay if one of Biggs cards didn't work. Recently he has separated Biggs operation from his own and has gotten extremely militant with how he moves.

Early one Tuesday morning Maddox was sitting alone at the long dining room table typing away in her miniature laptop. I sat down in the chair next to her as she let me in on her brilliant new idea. She explained how she is opening multiple bank accounts under air tight profiles we are not going to use for our "shit" and deposit her cash into those accounts. This new precaution was for a few reasons including not wanting to carry so much cash on her.

The next reason hit like a ton of bricks. "And I am splitting it up in multiple accounts incase something does ever happen. The feds like to freeze accounts and take away assets. If it isn't in anyones name around me they can't touch it." She reveals not taking her eyes away from the screen. "You expect something to happen?" I ask naively. We'd been on such a high I have forgotten what we do is illegal. Silly me. "A'maya I'll be real with you. Nothing in life is 100% and i'd rather be ready than sorry." She tells me.

Maddox goes on about setting me up a few accounts as well to protect our funds. She isn't doing this for everyone else in the house, just us. She is making these precautions before the "Big pay day" just incase anything does go left.

She then retrieves a box full of American Express gift cards. Maddox explains she set up dummy commerce websites for us both. We will sell items from the site using a ton of profiles but purchase everything with the gift cards. Even though the website host will take up to 7% we get to turn the cards into clean cash and retain majority of the value. Maddox explains cashing them out with a fence would only yield 60%. I decided to set up a website for my actual brand. Better get prepared for the next move asap. I helped her as we spent the day cashing out each Visa and American Express gift cards.

I was completely blown away to how smart and meticulous Maddox was when it came to her business. “Maddox you would be an asset to some fortune 500 company if you changed you path. Look how you think ahead, you’re a genius with numbers, you are good at marketing, you even design! Like come on.” I try to encourage her. “Chance. I have around 2.5 million saved up right now and I am going to make around 5.5 million dollars once we do this deal. What company is paying me that?” Maddox questions sweetly. I thought momentarily and I couldn’t answer her. She cut through the silence “None. I am not built to work under anyone in that capacity. I don’t work under anyone right now. These guys act like they are in charge but you see them fall apart when I’m not around.” Every word she spoke was true. “Aren’t you tired though?”

I genuinely inquired. Maddox stared at the floor for a moment then looked me in the eyes “This isn’t forever my friend. I told you after this job we are going home and opening that lounge you want. I didn’t forget.” My face lit up at just the mention of it. I got a snack for Maddox and I as we worked on the computer and mentally built the lounge in our minds using our imagination. She said she loves the idea so much she HAS to be a partner, especially being I am the only one she can trust. Maddox and I joked about her escape plan if it ever came down to it. She said if she could she would flee the country like she told me on the flight.

She promised to text me from WhatsApp an emoji of the flag of whatever country she was in. I laughed and told her I remember when she told me that on a flight. For a moment this felt more like getting prepared instead of joking. Maddox changed the subject and mentions how she and Amari still text but she's been distant because of the lifestyle. How he'd be the perfect man to marry but right now she's terrible with texting on her personal phone and is scared of commitment right now. Maddox has never gotten therapy for her enduring such horrific things and I had to ask what does she do to suppress it. "Money and Martini's!" She joked.

CHAPTER 21

Maddox and Biggs needed to make more money to fund their part of the "Big payday." J black negotiated they pay the $250,000 to his plug being that he bought the commissioner to the table. That part sounded fishy to me but whatever. All together they would be spending around half a million dollars if you include the office, renovations, profiles to look legit, wardrobes for everyone to play the part, and attending these banquet fund raiser dinners with the richest people in Southern California. "We need to get ready." Maddox announces to the girls.

We all knew that meant to go shopping for high retail items. The day was spent opening accounts at two Walmarts, two best buys and two different target stores. Five people getting approved for at least 15k a store got us to almost to over a half million dollars. I drove the rented Tahoe as the girls separated the gift cards in the back seat. Maddox notices a pair of apple headphones, and a few other items from the check out area on the floor near Tati. "When did you get a chance to buy all of this" she questions Tati. "I didn't" Tati laughs in her pothead fashion. "You stole this bullshit?" Maddox asks enraged. I see the smile melt off of Tati's face. "I took it off the shelf. I never get caught Maddie" she pleads.
"How dumb are you!? Tati stop smoking that got damn weed or stop working with us! Little bitch if you get me caught up over some petty theft I am going to break you neck!" Maddox screamed. "I won't I swear to god Maddie." "You bet not!" Maddox shot back coldly. I had never seen her this angry. I pulled over so we all can take a breather and reset the energy.

The rest of the day was spent mall hopping, opening accounts and racking up on high fashion. Tomorrow night was a fundraiser for the mayor and Biggs wanted us all in attendance. I knew the real reason he wanted us to go was to use these beautiful women he's around to entice these freaky older rich men.

At 10k a plate we had to look like a million dollars each. Ice took his girls shopping with pieces (cards) Biggs gave him. He wanted his stable to catch a few big fishes.

The next morning Maddox booked the best hair and make up artist in L.A to come to the house to get all of the girls ready. The sound of blow dryers, hip hop music playing from the tv and little discussions everywhere filled the room with life. You could hear the sound of the clippers in the next room from the barber Biggs booked for him and Ice. Ice pulls me to the side in the hallway. "You know I'm working tonight and my girls have to be there right?" He sincerely asks. I place my hand on his face. "Ice my baby, As much as we love being with each other we are not with each other. You are free to do whatever you want to." I could see the rage building in his eyes. "Here you go with this shit!" he exclaims. "What? Whats wrong?" I question. "I'm making all of these changes for you and you still want to play miss high and mighty. I didn't have the choice to have a normal childhood or normal mother like you! Mine sold her body and then died. If you want to keep sacrificing me for it go head, but only if it makes you feel better." He growls. I felt my heart drop and shame take over my body. He was more than right and I felt horrible for it. "I apologize. I just...Ok. And thank you for taking my feelings into consideration." I pleaded. He stared at me for a few seconds and walked away.
I asked myself was I crazy for getting turned on by him getting mad at me. I got so turned on as I stood with my back against the wall, right where he left me.

I couldn't believe the woman looking back at me from the mirror. I had dressed and had my make up done before but this is different. Having the top stylist that works for the stars polish you up brings out your best qualities. The diamond necklace from Kays I bought with my own money sparkled with each movement I made. My body sparkled from the Chanel shimmer body oil I rubbed all over my light coffee complexioned skin.

I slid into a black velvet dress that grabs my body in all the right places. Tight at the waist, low at the chest, soft as a whisper against my skin. One side of the neckline cuts higher with silver buckles that make it look a little dangerous with my shoulders out. The matching velvet gloves slide up to my elbows, and open toe Giuseppe Zanotti scrappy design completed the look. The whole thing felt like I'm dressed for trouble. The good kind.

We took tons of pictures in the driveway and in the car service on the way there. I stayed in deep thought about the decisions I have been making of lately. From this criminal enterprise I am now apart of to sleeping with a pimp. **A PIMP!** The more I thought the more I realized maybe I am toxic and love being in denial. Nobody made me feel like this man in my life before. I am just naturally afraid of everything that can come with. I need to take a std test! Lord please forgive me for all of this madness I have fallen into!

Maddox was quiet during the ride as well, typing away in her phone. I really prayed she find her way out of this all before it's too late. She is way to smart for what she gives herself. Her glow, her radiance could light up any room. Instead she chases darkness like she's ashamed of her own light.

The gated Baldwin hills estate had a driveway full of rolls royces, bentleys and black Suvs either parked to the side or dropping guest off. After 8 months of mansion hopping you would think I would have gotten used to the houses by now, but they never ceased to amaze me. Yeah, they all have the same amenities but sometimes you come across something so grand it takes your breath away. The 1st floor was filled with prominent, wealthy people in their finest black tie attire. I grabbed a glass of champagne from one the servers and went to explore alone. Phony laughter of men and women who needed a deal done bounced off of the walls while jazz music from the live band kept the room alive. I stopped at a pink and black painting of four inverted Marilyn Monroes in different squares.

"You know who that is?" A young well dressed, toffee complexioned man asks as he stands next to me with his glass of champagne. He had a low cut, clean shaven and his muscles almost bust out of his three piece suit. "Marylin Monroe?" I respond almost confused. "Well yes and no. That is her but this painting is by the great Andy Warhol. Just sold for 5.7 million dollars." He responds with his eyes still stuck on the painting in awe. "And how do you know that?" I ask and take a sip of my champagne. "I just bought it." He asserts as he takes a sip from his glass. "Oh excuse me. So this is your home?" I ask. "No you're fine. Well no you are fine but you are... never mind and yes this is my home." He laughs between words. His game was corny but there was something magnetic about him. "Charles Winfield" He asserts with his hand extended. "A.." I almost gave my real name but remembered promptly where we were. "Cynthia Dunbar" I respond with a smile. "For a minuet there I almost thought you forgot your name." He quips back. "Cut it out. I was just blown away by everything at once. I froze up. Don't get used to it." I joke. "Well I could get used to a lot of things with you Cynthia" Charles says softly and turns in my direction. I froze up for real this time. I wasn't expecting to meet this gorgeous man let alone the owner of this beautiful estate. See what happens when you hang in the right places? I thought to myself. Oh wait a minuet I'm here on a mission! "Well Charles I'm pretty sure your wife would not appreciate that." I reply slyly. "I know she wouldn't ,I'm not married. I actually single." He replies. "Yeah and i'll also buy the bridge you have for sale" I answer with a grin. "Ha !you're funny. No I am telling you the truth, scouts honor..." As he continued to try to convince me of his bachelor life I caught Ice out the side of my eye over Charles's shoulder watching us as he sipped from a snifter glass. Even across the room I could see his anger building. For some reason it turned me on and I wanted to add fuel to his fire. I pretended to laugh harder at Charles jokes and lightly touch his arm whenever he told a corny one.

Charles walked with me room to room introducing me to so many people and told them about the fictitious company I worked for. Maddox could been seen in a corner surrounded by wealthy men, hypnotized by her beauty hanging on her every word. Sabrina had the same effect. Tonight she looked like a goddess and nothing like her erotic profession. Unsurprisingly most of the men in the room knew who she was, and if they weren't with their wives they followed her like a moth to a flame. Babydoll who looked equally as gorgeous spent the evening entertaining one man like me, as Biggs used the commissioner to introduce him to all the power players in the room. Ice looked edible in his tailored black Armani suit and all of his girls looked amazing. We all worked the room with different intentions but either way they were all fucked. I felt like a lion amongst my pride in a room full of prey.

Charles kept my attention all night with stories and jokes that were so corny I was forced each laugh. I didn't want to seem like we came to his party nine people deep so I told him I am here by myself tonight to make connections in a new city. I hate myself for not knowing something was up when that look in his eye changed. I assumed it was because he found me attractive. I just didn't know how much he did and how bad he wanted me.

The next drink we took together he went to the bar to get personally. He informs me that this is his special recipe and orders it at every bar. Amoretto sour, extra shot, no eggs. I wasn't a big drinker and really enjoyed the sweetness of it. Charles walks us back by the pool area claiming to want to be able to hear our conversation better. When I sat down on a chaise lounge I felt this heaviness take over my head. My equilibrium went out of wack and I couldn't keep my eyes balanced. "Charles I don't feel right." I fought to say on my now locking up jaw. A tsunami of sweat rushes out of my pores and covers my whole body as I fight to keep my eyes open. "Charles...no" I mutter with my jaw clenched. He calmly watched, pretending to help me lay down as he fondled my breast. "Here lay down Cynthia." He whispers as his creepy voice goes in and out while breathing heavily. He began to slide his hand up my thigh and I couldn't resist.

My core had turned in complete cement as I became a prisoner in my own body. Thank God Ice is crazy about me and vowed to knock out anyone who touches me. He was in that house furious all night but remained professional. The fact that I went missing with some stranger drove him nuts. He tried to wait for us to return but each minuet drove him closer to insanity. He searched the house until he saw on the chair with Charles on top of me. He rushed outside and immediately saw the state I was in. Ice swung and punched Charles in the mouth. Charles stumbled but didn't have enough time before Ice threw another two piece. I guess he wasn't going to let anyone get a second to recuperate like he gave Brian. Charles fell to the floor. Ice jumped on top of him like a mad man. "You drugged her you dirty muthafucka!" He yelled as he swung blow for blow against a now defenseless Charles. Whatever he slipped into my drink made it impossible for me to get up and stop Ice even if I wanted to. Biggs and Maddox rushed in the backyard as Maddox closed the door behind them.

Biggs rushes over and grabs Ice off of Charles as Maddox rushes to my side. Everyone is screaming. "What the fuck?" Biggs yells at Ice. "He drugged her! Look at her!" Ice screams pointing at me as Maddox yells "What happened to my girl?" Biggs instructs Maddox to watch the door. He turns to Charles laying in a fetal position on the ground and kicks him hard in the stomach. Biggs leans down, lifts his head up and whispers "You dirty muthafucka you are going to pay for this. Not today but I am coming real soon for your ass." Then bangs Charles head on the hard concrete. "Maddox get the girls and meet us out front." Biggs instructs as Ice picks my limp, lifeless body up off of the furniture. He carries me to the car from the side of the house and places me in the back seat. I blacked out.

Me getting drugged for the 1st time ever was a nightmare for me but a dream come true for Biggs. Charles turned out to be the city manager and that makes him 3rd in command. Biggs set in motion a blackmail play to get whatever he wanted especially when it came to getting whatever permits he needed for this building. He leveraged the attempted SA against Charles to meet more investors and ensure we get loans. Ice and I have been sleeping and waking up to each other in the mornings since the incident.

I do not remember how we got home or how I even got in the bed. Apparently my night in shining armor carried me, and dressed me for bed. He couldn't leave me in that state and decided to cuddle with me. Even as I slept he protected me. Ice wanted to get more revenge on Charles outside of financial. He was beyond furious and spoke about it damn near everyday. That ass whooping wasn't enough in his eyes and he vowed to get revenge. Here was this man who protects me, tries to change his life for me, and willing to risk his freedom. My own father wasn't willing to do that for me. I was drowning in love and there wasn't anything I could do about it.

CHAPTER 22

Besides that disgusting encounter I had that banquet was a success. I still questioned whether or not I should press charges. Biggs assured me he would make Charles pay up. Maddox met tons of different mangers of huge hedge funds and floated the idea to Biggs to maybe do more than one building. His only discretion was if J black would want a piece of everything they do. He expressed that they are lucky they don't have to pay for protection now that the gang bangers know they are in town getting money. If they stay too long and get too comfortable there's a chance that may change.

I gotta give it to him. Biggs was a visionary and saw every play before it happened. He was greedy but he wasn't glutton. We all continued working in the stores doing the instant credit profiles. By now Maddox had perfected it and drove up and down the state of California and Oregon. From Portland to San Diego.

If they had a retail store that had a place we could stop and get money, we hit that town. Some places we visited we'd be the only black people for miles. Thank god we worked during the day because I wouldn't want to be caught at night round these places.

It was February 1st when Brian finally texted me. From everything I have experienced on top of working and studying for my role I honestly forgot about him. You still mad at me? he texted. I couldn't help but to feel sorry for him. I used him as a rebound, let him catch feelings knowing damn well I couldn't have them back. And him actually standing up to Ice made him more attractive. No Brian. How are you? I sent back with a kissy face emoji. We texted the back and forth the whole time my crew took our road trips. Ice would texted and my heart would melt. Brian would text and I would get butterflies. I am in no player in any sense of the word but damn this was fun. Brian asked me to be his valentine which threw me for a loop. One, I am shocked Ice hadn't asked and two he's still interested in me. I told him yes without even thinking. I had to tell Maddox what was going on in my love life because it was too much for me. She warned me that I was playing a dangerous game because Ice was head over heels for me. Maddox informed me of private discussions they had about him changing his life around to really be with me. I confessed that I was in love with him but I couldn't be with him
Until he completely left that life alone. I fee bad about his upbringing but I won't bring myself down to that. I deserve better.

Back in Malibu Biggs and Maddox finally got their share of the money to pay the commissioner and get the paper work started. He knew for certain everything would go through especially since his new buddy Charles was going to sign off on everything. They began bringing people by the bogus store front office we whipped together. Biggs hired actors from craigslist to stop by the office and play potential clients when he had meetings with investors. He didn't bring Ice or Maliak into the play but promised Ice $500,000 from his cut. I sat in an office we decorated with pictures of me photoshopped with a fake family.

Anytime he would bring someone into my office I would pretend to be on an important international call and didn't have time to speak. I'd wave and make up some random name, thanking for speaking to me so late because of the time difference. Gathering the paperwork and courting investors took a couple weeks but everything started taking shape.

Unbeknownst to me Pepsi and Tati still hung out. Biggs knew but figured it was ok because she hooked us up with J black and it lead to money. I still didn't trust Pepsi but held a ton of empathy for her. I remember Pepsi telling me her heartbreaking story on how she got to L.A. She was back in Houston in a abusive relationship with a powerful drug dealer. He would beat her mercilessly in front of their 3 year old son. One day when he was pistol whipping her the gun went off and their son was hit with a stray bullet. The father got a light sentence and terrorized her for testifying against him. She left Texas with one suitcase. She met J black at a party and they got cool ever since. She met Ice and damn near everybody else the same way. I don't mix tragedy with trust and kept my eye out on her.

It's been 3 days and no one had heard from Tati. I started to get worried because she was still dealing with that abusive, married baseball player. I was scared he did something to her. We stayed the course, in the office everyday and acting like a legit company. Tati rushes in the office and bust in my office. "We gotta talk" she says as she closes the door. Tati goes on to tell me she and Pepsi were at the target on Figueroa and got caught stealing dumb shit. She gets searched and they find a ton of gift cards. She explains she just had a huge baby shower to try to explain it. They get locked up and held for 3 days. That wasn't the problem. She told me before she left this morning the same guy that Ice fought that day came in asking her a bunch of questions. He knew about us being a crime ring and wanted to know where Biggs was. He didn't have much information but tried to get dirt on Ice real hard, and inquired about Maddox. Tati didn't call collect in fear they will trace the phone number. She told him bullshit information to throw off their scent and vowed to work for him if they let her go.

She claimed to have promised not to tell the rest of us. Tati took two trains and 3 cabs to make sure she wasn't being followed before coming here. He had information but was fishing to put the pieces together. I sat there listening in complete shock. How long had Brian been playing me?
Was he stringing me along this whole time. I called Maddox into the office and Tati recalled the entire story for her without skipping a beat. When Tati was done with the story Maddox slapped her faster than lightning. "You dumb bitch! I told you dont bring us down with this low class, hood rat, petty theft bullshit. This is why we keep Pepsi away from us!
She is bad luck" She yelled and went to hit her again as Tati put up her hands to protect her face. "Wait a minuet Maddox. This could be good." I interrupt. I explain that I had no idea who Brain was but now his cover is blown. He doesn't have much information which is another good thing. Now that we know we must move accordingly. Brian didn't tell me who he was and don't forget he asked me to be his valentine. I got a trick up my sleeve he'll never see coming.

At the house we discussed what happened to Tati at the round table and what our next move should be. Ice scolded me for bringing the cop into our circle. I defended myself because I never actually bought him around anybody. I met him on a flight. How could he know about the rest of ya'll? Biggs informed everyone its time to devise an escape plan for when this deal is done. Ice asked what are we going to do about Pepsi, because we don't know what she told the police and how could we even find out. Tati would have to talk to her and sees what she says. We laid out step by step on how to handle Brian and get the big play done. Maddox suggested moving to another house but Biggs didn't want the gang bangers to get the idea they move a lot and start feeling uneasy. That made perfect sense, and we all agreed. Ice was going to lay low and not get seen with us at all. Biggs suggested we all get new cell phones and I switch out mine after my "date" with Brian. He told Tati to keep Pepsi at arms length but keep her away from the house. He regretted not listening to Ice when he told him to get rid of her completely.

I honestly couldn't help but to feel stupid. How could I let him rock me to sleep like this. I am not too street savvy but I at least should be able to see a cop from a mile away. Maddox reassured me I didn't lead them to us but I still felt uneasy leading up to the date. Anger built up inside of me at the thought of this geek trying to outsmart me. When did he start watching us? What would make him start investigating the crew so much? It couldn't have been over a damn fight. Tati was dumb for stealing and I still don't know what Pepsi told them. My head was spinning for days. I missed Ice but understood we couldn't see each other until the coast was clear. We would communicate through WhatsApp and fall asleep on FaceTime. No more text or calls on the regular phone. Ice revealed he was jealous I had a valentine that wasn't him even if it was a pig. The distance between us somehow made us grow closer.

I stayed on the phone with him as he made his runs. He told me how he would retire and hand the business over to Maliak. He would ask where would we settle together and swore he spent cold winters in NYC before. His personality began to change and he started to be more carefree. Ice looked as though some weight had been lifted off of his shoulders and he finally found his propose. I told him about my lounge and we would trade ideas on a name to use.

The morning of valentines day I woke up in complete panic mode. So many emotions rushed through my mind. I was scared because I planned on tying up an officer of the law. Then I would get mad all over again remembering how he played me. How I shared my body with this deceitful, lying, jerk. Brian and I texted all day and I convinced him it would be better if I cooked dinner and we ate at his house. Brian agreed. I couldn't but help to remember the time he kept asking about my living situation. Is that when he began snooping around? The anticipation was building.

Maddox gave me a prep talk over breakfast and drilled in my head all of the questions I was to ask him. Biggs was cool as a fan and explained this isn't his first rodeo with the law. They can sniff around all they want as long as they don't find anything. The day this deal is done we all leave California behind. Brian wanted to spend lunch together and surprise me with more activities. I was nervous he would trick me and arrest me on the spot. I erased everyones contact and messages from my phone just incase. I got prepared to switch roles with the police and I do the interrogating.

I took a uber and met Brian at a nice restaurant in the Weho area of LA. The streets were vibrant and full of life. I did my best playing it cool and not show my true intent. He carried on the day smiling, clueless to what I had planned. Brian locked his hand with mine as we walked down the street. This what true deceit and betrayal felt like. He filled the day with rollerskating and go kart racing. If he wasn't a back stabbing snake this date would have been perfect. The hatred I had for this main slowly cooked like beef in a crockpot. We headed to trader joes and got the ingredients I needed for tonights meal. I purposely picked up 3 bottles of Pinot Grigio. The plan was to get him drunk off of his rocker then strike.

I cooked as he played oldies music like Marvin Gaye, Teddy Pendergrass and Micheal Jackson album cuts. Brian had tea light candles set all over his apartment and rose petals leading from the kitchen to his bedroom. He bought chocolate hearts, a huge teddy bear and a dozen roses for me. Did he have the same plan I had for tonight and being deceptive? Until I knew exactly what was going on I played nice.

We laughed over dinner and I told him I wanted to open a lounge back home. I wasn't cut out for California and I think Ive over stayed my welcome. It was like he was agreeing with his face. "Well I am going to miss you. When do you plan on leaving?" He questions as he finishes his 3rd glass of wine. I filled it back up before he could think. "You trying to take advantage of me tonight?" He jokes as he takes another gulp. "You have no idea." I respond in a seductive tone. We finished the small dinner I prepared from premade dishes from trader joes. I just added a few spices and a couple extra ingredients. Brian was so distracted he just noticed I hadn't touched my glass of wine yet. "Wait a minuet. Why are you still babysitting your 1st glass?" He slurs. By now my tolerance has grown so I knew 1 glass of wine wouldn't hurt. I haven't had a drink since the night at Charles's house. Just the thought of it gave me the chills. I downed my glass in one setting and refilled it. I knew I wasn't going to have another glass, but he didn't. "Baby put on some music, let me dance for you." I say in my best seductive voice. He passes me the phone to choose what I want to hear. I play *Would you mind* by Janet Jackson.

He sits on the couch as I turn down all of the lights. I began to strip for him slowly, rubbing each part of my body as I passed it. I wore a sexy red and black two piece la pearla lingerie set. When he would try to touch me I would swat his hands away. I played *Peaches and Cream* by Monifah next, sat on the other end of the couch and began pleasing myself. Brian got so aroused he couldn't control himself. He leapt over to my side like an experienced house cat. "No." I whisper and push him back with one leg on his chest. I could see his manhood through his sweat pants fully erect. I moaned louder and rubbed faster with my legs in the air as I rock my body whispering his name. Brian watches like a mad man unsure on what to do. I climax down my ass checks, put some on my finger and wipe it on his lips. I head over to his bedroom. Brian jumps off the coach and follows me blindly.

"Baby can we spice'n it up a little tonight?" I ask. "Whats on your mind baby." He desperately asked. I could tell by his face I could do ANYTHING under the sun to him at this point. I went over to the bag I bought and pulled out handcuffs, a whip, blind fold, whip cream and a bondage gag ball. "Oh shiiiiiiit! We getting freaky tonight!" He says excitedly.
I lead him over to the bed to remove his t-shirt. Brian had no concept of romance and ripped his clothes off like they were on fire. His erect manhood swinging in the air fully

ready. He lays down and I apply whip cream to his chest. He moans uncontrollably as I slowly lick it off while I rubbing between his legs. That one glass of wine didn't get me drunk but it has me fully aroused. The sex energy in the air made my whole body hot. I looked down at this man who I almost caught feelings for. One thing about Brian. He was not lacking in the downstairs department and knew how to use it. I need to feel him one more time before I say goodbye. He placed a condom on and got on top of me and did a slow grind to the r&b playlist playing in the background. Brian hit every spot to drive me wild. I scratched up his back and yelled his name as I came back to back. When it was his turn to climax I convinced him to let me tie him up and blindfold him. Blinded by passion he agreed.

I handcuffed his hands to the bed post and used the rope to separately tie up his feet at the end on the bed. "Oh I like this." He groans as his body searches for mine. I remove the leather whip from my bag and stuck him as hard as possible. "Ouch! Whoa baby thats a little hard." He yelps. "Fuck you!" I yell and start swinging the whip faster and faster across his naked body. He squealed and tried to move away from the direction the whip came from. "A'maya i don't like this shit!" He yells so hard the veins are popping out of his neck. I rip the blindfold off. "Fuck you Pig!" I spit in his face and start wielding the whip fast again all over his body. "Ok ok ok wait let me explain" He pleads. I told him I want to know everything from the beginning.

Brian explains that he's been onto Biggs for some time now and he lead them to Maddox. That flight where he sat next to be was fully orchestrated. At first he thought I could be a lead but then he started to like me. He made sure my name was taken out of the investigation. It's been hard catching them because they move so much and haven't been arrested yet. He knew Tati was down with them so took the one chance he had to try to get information. He saw that I was doing parties and wasn't involved with them. I asked back to back questions from A to Z. I told him how he broke my heart playing me like this. It wasn't true at all but I was devastated he was so deceptive. Brian pleaded with me. I asked when are they planning on arresting anyone. He swore they are still building a case but Biggs baby mother is cooperating. They caught them at the airport when they left LA a few months ago. The agency is after Biggs for Ponzi schemes, identity theft and a laundry list of felonies. He explained that if I gave Biggs any idea of our discussion he will have to come after me and add me to the indictment. I asked is there anyway to let Maddox go and get Biggs. Brian explained even if she testifies against him she still has to do some time for being the mastermind. I asked what did Pepsi say to the cops. He told me she stayed solid and played dumb.

When I couldn't think of any more questions I got dressed and gathered my things. "Hello? I answered everything are you going to untie me? You can't fuck me then leave me like this A'maya" He pleaded again. I walked over, put the key on the night table and spit in his face again. "You used me. You used my body. You are a predator Brian. I hate you and I swear to god I pray no one comes in here and finds you. Add me to any investigation you want! I'm pretty sure sleeping with your suspects, wining and dining them is apart of the job description. You are a low human being and you disgust me." I snarl. He yells my name louder and louder while yanking the handcuffs trying to break free as I exit.

CHAPTER 23

Back at the house everyone was in anticipation over what news I'll come back with. Tati was right they don't have enough to make an arrest right now. I gave them the history on how I even got on his radar and was relieved I didn't the police to everyone here. I kept the sex part to myself and plan to take that to the grave. I laughed at the memory of him naked, erect manhood in the air, screaming for me to untie him. Even though he answered all of my questions I still didn't trust him and I still don't trust Pepsi. "It's just a sign we are over staying our welcome baby. Lets get paid and hit the highway." Biggs smoothly says. I had already transferred the money I made out here to my website and various accounts. I wish I kept it in bitcoin from back then. Maddox was buying profiles on the dark web when they were $10 a coin. Biggs informed everyone that showtime was near and its time to get in our places.

Maddox created air tight profiles with great credit scores to apply for the loans and to get money from hedge fund investors. When they researched the company or any individual with us they would see outstanding reviews with the better business bureau and outstanding credit lines. The stage was set. In 3 days Biggs is scheduled to finalize the paperwork and they do a wire transfer. That evening Tati and Pepsi was hanging out smoking ,as usual, under the Hollywood sign. Pepsi had already assured Tati she didn't tell the police anything. In a moment of transparency Pepsi told Tati what true plans J black had brewing. 30 million dollars will make anyone lose their minds. Apparently J black planned to wait for the transfer go through and somehow kidnap them all and extort the whole sum for themselves. J black didn't have the profiles or funds to ever make something like this go through. He's greedy and untrustworthy. Tati questioned Pepsi if she knew that, why would she introduce them to us. Pepsi explained initially it was for revenge and then they looked like they were going to make money together so she let everything slide.

Now she feels bad because J black is planning on beating someone to death for that money if he has too. Pepsi begged Tati to tell Biggs but don't say her name or bring her into it. The gang bangers will kill her for sure if they knew she was repeating it. Tati drove Pepsi right to Maddox and Biggs to figure out what to do. "What the fuuuuuck!" Maddox exclaimed. "Why can't I get a break with you people?" "What you mean by you people?" Biggs asked. "Oh fuck you Biggs. You know exactly what I mean! You people! A'maya kissing cops, Ice beating up cops, Tati and Pepsi get arrested by cops and you leading me to the cops!" Maddox yells and pounds on the kitchen table. "Now I have to worry about the gangbangers you HAD to bring into our lives! Only god knows how much of that is left because Biggs thirsty ass couldn't wait until I got back from new york!" Maddox screamed at the top of her lungs. She yelled so loudly her face was turning dark red and her veins were protruding from her neck. Everyone spoke up at once trying to defend themselves "I don't want to fucking hear it! A bunch of nitwits acting like amateurs. I'm going out by myself and want be alone!" She yells then points her finger in Biggs direction. "Fix this shit. NOW" She walks to the table, grabs her pocketbook and leaves the house. Everyone was so silent you could hear the engine on the truck start and Maddox drive off. I know she's mad, and I only caught a stray because I was there but damn did that hurt. Pepsi was a bad omen and I knew I didn't like her. Biggs was dumb to connect with her people and truthfully he bought this all on himself. I am not a scammer and nobody taught me the ropes. I couldn't wait until I boarded the plane back to New York City. This west coast life been too much for me.

Today was game day. The plan was to close the office after deal was done, have our bags packed and move to a hotel downtown. They would expect us to be in 5 star hotels so we would go to lower brand hilton hotels. Maddox switched out the SUV for a completely different one. Biggs and Maddox decided to keep the whole 30 million and split it amongst each other. Each girl would get a million a piece now. Maddox and Biggs stood to walk away with 13 million a piece. My heart pounded all day just thinking about everything about to take place.

I wore my business casual skirt set, Chanel pin, with hair up in a bun. We dropped our suitcases off before the meeting and headed to the office. "Places everyone" Biggs cheers and claps his hands. "Daddy you still gonna love me when you're rich?" Sabrina asks Biggs seductively . "Baby I been rich. Now go hop on them phones we got a show to do." He slaps her butt then heads to his office. Within 20 minuets a group of business men walk in the front door lead by the commissioner.. My stomach turned at the sight of Charles.

We caught eye contact as I was closing the door to my office. Shame flushed his as he cleared his throat and played cool. Biggs welcomed them into his office and offered them all celebratory cigars for the occasion.

The gentlemen cheered as each one of them signed the paper work. Baby doll bought in a bottle ace of spades Biggs requested. He called all of the employees and hired actors into his office to toast to the new deal! They started the wire transfer right in front of me as I fought not to faint. 30 million dollars being transfer into an account of some I knew personally was mind-blowing . After the meeting everyone scheduled to go the commercial building on Monday and start the ball rolling.

Little did they know they'd see Jesus before they ever see us again. Within 5 minuets of them leaving J Black and 4 of his goos storm in the front door. "How we looking baby?" He asks walking with his arms in the air, wearing a threatening smile. "We good!" Biggs replies nervous but excitedly. "We good!?" J black yells. "We good!" Biggs yells back jumping up and down. "So where's my money homie?" J black asks as the smile melts off is face. "We finalized the paperwork today. They started the transfer. Takes 2-3 business days for something that large!" Biggs lied through his teeth. "Let's go out a celebrate partner!" Biggs shouts testing J blacks temperature. J black slowly smiles again "Yea I know you ain't dumb enough to run off with that bread. We'd kill all yall." J black jokes and for the 1st time his goons broke their stone cold faces and laughed with him. The rest of us laughed uncomfortably. "Don't even think like that my boy! We locked in for life my brother." Biggs laughs with them. I didn't take that threat lightly and was glad we planned a step ahead. "Where yall trying to party Biggs?" J black inquires. "How about back at the house? We about to head there now. Give us a little while to get changed, pull up and we get it in." Biggs replies. "Nah man, I'm following you there. Im not letting you out of my sight!" J black vocalizes. "Ok baby however you feel." Biggs says cooly. I knew whatever the new plan was, we would have to discuss it in the car. "Let us lock up the office and meet you in front. You follow us back to the crib." J black was hesitant but agreed.

We grabbed everything we could carry and ran out the back door. Maddox hopped behind the wheel and told the rest of us to duck down. They were busy looking for a black SUV and didn't even pay attention to the white pick up truck pulling out and going the opposite direction. Within 6 minuets Biggs phone was ringing back to back. He rolls down the passenger window and throws his phone out. Maddox and the rest of us followed suit. Baby doll grabbed new burners for each us out of a Walmart bag and passed them around. "What about Pepsi?" Tati asks.

The car was silent as everyone thought. "When we get to the hotel I'll give you some money for her. Tell her to leave town tonight if she could."

At the hilton we got connecting rooms on the top floor. Maddox and Biggs gave Tati 50k a piece to give to Pepsi and told her to be safe. The energy was high but anxious. "We can't stay here Biggs. I got a place we could hide out in San Francisco, let's leave town from here and regroup. I don't even feel safe spending a night here to be honest with you." Maddox explained. "Let's leave first thing in the morning. Like 6 am." He replies. "I'd rather leave when its pitch black. He doesn't know what car we are in lets get out of here. At least go up to Tarzana where ice is." Maddox suggested. Biggs agreed.

As we waited to hear from Tati, Maddox transferred everyone's money to their respected accounts. "Daddy I can't wait until we make love on a bed of money." Sabrina moans when her phone alerts her of the deposit. All I could think about is hopping on a flight and leaving this godforsaken place. Maybe I will return one day under different circumstances but currently I must flee.

Tati finally called in a panic. "They got her!" She yells into the phone. "Who?" Biggs pleads. Tati pulled up just as they were dragging Pepsi out of her house by her hair. Tati watched helplessly from the truck as they forcefully pushed Pepsi into a black camero with dark tinted windows. Tati rushed back across town to us.

As soon as Tati pulled up we all rushed to pack the truck as soon as possible. Who cares how much money you have if you are not alive to spend it. Biggs drove in the direction of Ice's house in Tarzana, also considered the valley. Tati's phone rang from Pepsi's contact. "Put that muthafucka Biggs on the phone!" He yelled form the other end. J black was at the house and we never showed up. He had Pepsi and threatened to kill her if we didn't show up. Biggs tried to tell him its all a misunderstanding but J black was a mad man.

J black kept yelling and there was no calming him down. He yelled I'm not playing with you and then you heard a loud pop and something heavy thud. "Yea now she's dead! You're next if you don't show up with my bread!" J black screamed then hung up. The truck was silent as Biggs drove. "Its too late now. There's nothing we can do. Keep driving Biggs." Maddox coldly chimed in. Here rode a car full of millionaires not sure if they'll stay alive long enough to spend it.

CHAPTER 24

I ran into Ice's arms as soon as he opened the door. I was overwhelmed with emotions. Scared, excited about the money, and upset they did Pepsi like that. We all walked in Ice's modest home he's renting as he walked around the room moving things to make us all comfortable.

"What happened yall?" I asked in full shock. Maddox gives him the full details on the role Pepsi played and how they tried to save her but didn't get to her in time. Maliak arrives in the middle of the confusion. "Aye yall. The word is out with every crip in California there's a green light on yall heads. J black has every airport in the state under full surveillance and send goons to Vegas." Maliak proclaims. Biggs sat and listened intently. "Did they say anything about San Francisco or Portland?" Biggs asked while still recalculating his next move. "I ain't hear nothing about Portland but I don't know if I would trust staying in Cali at all." He expressed with his eye brows raised.

I have been afraid before but never in my life have I felt this amount of fear before. Our lives depended on what moves we decided to make tonight.

Maddox, Ice, Biggs and I sat at the kitchen table looking at maps and trying to figure out the best route to leave. Maddox suggested the airport in Boise, Idaho may seem the safest route. It's about a 13-14 hour ride but we could do it with everyone taking turns behind the wheel. By now it's 1:30 a.m and we contemplated if we should leave now or 1st thing in the morning.

If we left right now we could be in Reno, Nevada around 6 or 7 a.m. We could rest there for a few hours and then head to Idaho from there.

Maddox decided the Peppermill resort spa and casino would be the best choice. Ice went to start packing and Biggs stopped him. He told him how he couldn't come with us because this wasn't his fight. It wouldn't be safe to leave me behind with Ice because he can't protect me against all of them. Ice shouldn't come with us incase we need him to help from the outside. Plus no one has seen Ice involved with this situation so it was best to keep him out of it. Ice wouldn't hear none of it. He would not let me face this danger alone. Maliak left and came back with a Mercedes sprinter van to leave town in. I began crying for more reasons than I can pinpoint. Ice kissed me as my tears soaked both of our faces. "We're going to be ok baby I promise." Ice reassures me. He was assigned designated driver because Biggs is correct, no one has seen him. I put my hair in a ponytail and wore a dad hat pulled down low. We stopped at in and out burger to load up on food and hit the road.

We arrived in the small desert town around 7 a.m got two suites and unpacked. Ice and I slept longer than the rest of the crew from the drive up. Maddox worked diligently to find us flights as Biggs made calls the check the temperature in L.A. The streets are looking for them and J black even put a bounty out on us. The news gave me instant anxiety but I remained cool just like everyone else. Maddox was able to book everyone flights to their destination but they all are leaving tomorrow. The thought of one more day made me uneasy. I didn't know how everyone remained so cool while being on the run. Just stay out of sight and we will be ok.

Tati and Ice smoked joint after joint, Maddox worked on her laptop as Biggs entertained Baby doll and Sabrina. "Aye this is getting boring. How about we hit a few slots downstairs?" Biggs asks followed by his grin. "I think we should stay out of sight Biggs." Ice chimes in between pulls of his joint. "We are hundreds of miles out sight. Those LA bangers are looking for us in California. Vegas and phoenix even. Not up here." He laughs.

I didn't know if he wanted to go downstairs out of sheer boredom, stupidity or honestly believed we were out of harms way. Maybe a piece of Biggs was tired of running and wanted to get caught. I didn't agree with his idea at all but he can be so persuasive. "Biggs sit ya ass down and let's get out of here tomorrow morning." Maddox jumps in the discussion. "Look. You scarecrows can stay holed up in this room if you want to. I am taking my ladies to get something to eat and play a few hands of blackjack. I keep my head on a swivel baby and I'm slicker than oil." Biggs affirms as he walks towards the door with Baby doll and Sabrina in tow. The door slams behind them.

"I am not going to jail on account of his dumb shit. And I damn sure refuse to get shot for him. If we are staying here this long I am going to look for flights out of the airport right here. What yall wanna do?" Maddox asks the rest of us. Poor Tati's life has just been upended and she has no idea what to do or where to go. "Maddox I don't have anywhere to go. I don't know anyone anywhere." Tati utters. "I don't feel sorry for you Tatiana. You are a millionaire. Pick a city and start over." Maddox responds coldly. "Miami, I guess." Tati vents. Maddox the next hour getting Tati a sport cars, an apartment in a high-rise in Miami under an airtight profile and booked her flight for 8:45 p.m tonight. Less then 6 hours away. Of course she charged Tati for everything. I still didn't trust Tati fully but I felt bad for her. I wanted her to have a fresh start and really live out her life. No more scamming, married men and living on the run. I prayed everything worked out for her.

Maddox then turned her sights on me "What you and Ice going to do?" She asked. We had never discussed things that far in advance. I know Ice has his life set up out here and can't just pack up and run. He and Biggs figure he isn't in immediate danger because J Black only met him that one time at the Casino. Ice made it a habit to not be seen when they worked on this new endeavor. "Can you give us a minuet?"

I ask Maddox and lead Ice to the next room. "Baby I really think you should stay here and straighten your life out. You have a lot going on and I am caught up in this crap. We can come back together when the smoke clears." I try to convince him as my eyes began to water. "A'maya, baby I would love to come with you. But you are right. And I am not ready. There is a certain way I want things to be for us to be together and it isn't this way." He explained. I knew this was the way things had to be but my heart still shattered into pieces as he spoke. " Just give me time to get right." He said with such sadness in his eyes. "You should leave immediately then. Maddox is booking flights as we speak. You have the truck go now." I told him. Ice thought momentarily and agreed. He kissed me so passionately it felt like a good bye kiss. I would need to get out of here and we could meet anywhere. I believed Ice would switch paths and do the right thing. Biggs had already transferred what he promised him and all Ice had to do was figure out his purpose.

Maddox booked my flight to go home scheduled for 10:08 tonight. I opted out of the sky rise apartment and car she offered. With almost two million dollars I don't mind putting everything in my own name. Ice wanted to wait until Biggs returned to tell him his plans. I wished he would of listened to me to hit the road.

While we planned our departure in the hotel room, Biggs and the girls went to Squeeze in Breakfast and Lunch. They operated like there wasn't a care in the world. They underestimated the reach and the danger posed by having an issue with J black had held. J black sent pictures of the crew to all of the gangbangers statewide and even posted them on social media with a bounty attached. And in this day and age you can't identify who is apart of their faction because they don't wear identifying colors like back in the day. Biggs never held a chance.

The black and majority grey haired man sat a few tables away from the crew as they sat in complete bliss. He confirmed on his phone it was them by confirming it twice. He sent a picture of the three unsuspecting victims to J black. Within a few moments an alert came on across the man's screen confirming a wire transfer of 50k to his account. J black then instructed him to follow them back to wherever they were staying. Who knew within 8 hours our world would be flipped upside down. The man got in his Lincoln town car and followed them back to the hotel once they left breakfast.

When they returned Biggs and the girls took showers to get dressed. He claimed he wanted to see the town and blow off some steam. "Would you sit you fat ass down for a minuet! This is serious Biggs!" Ice yelled. "Damn lil bro. Being around these females got you emotional. You know we've faced bigger monsters. Relax." Biggs exhales cooly. "How about this? We stay in the hotel and just gamble. We will be right downstairs. Deal?" He asks and exits without a response from anyone. He didn't even give anyone enough time to tell him the updated plans. "Ill stay take you to the airport and then leave. I just want to make sure you're safe. If you leave at 10 ill drop you off at 8." Ice says as he rolls up another joint. That still would not be early enough.

Tati prepared herself to leave. Maddox instructed her to call a taxi and take it from the EVS urgent care parking lot to avoid being seen in the front of the hotel. When she landed in Miami send a message through WhatsApp to let us know she's good. Maddox was forward thinking like that and decided thats the exit we will all leave from. Ice left the room to park the car closest to that exit for showtime. We gave each other hugs and Tati left the room. I prayed for her safe travels and sat with my anxiety.

I tried taking a nap but it really was just time well spent laying in Ice's arms. We basked in silence for a while not knowing what to expect. The 6:30 p.m alarm we set blasted in the room to remind us it was time to go. Maddox and I brushed our teeth, took showers and got our bags prepared to go. Ice left the room with our bags at 7:45 p.m to get the car and meet us at the exit.

Unbeknownst to us Biggs played craps with Baby doll on one arm and Sabrina on the other. He was winning so much money he drew a crowd around him that was cheering him on. "Which one of my babies is the lucky one?" He yelled out jokingly and held the dice in front of Sabrina to blow on them. He threw the dice and hit 7. The crowd roared. "Wait a minuet Wait a minuet!" He screamed with a smile and held the dice in front of Baby doll. She blew on the dice, he threw them and hit 11. The crowd erupted in a cheer once more. Biggs was on such a high he didn't see the trouble rolling in.

J black swiftly approached from the right of the casino with four gang members like one of those speed walkers. "Aye homie you thought I wouldn't find you" He yelled out as he swung and hit Biggs in the jaw. The guys started throwing punches until Biggs fell as all of the people around the table screamed and scattered. Two other gang bangers approached and grabbed Sabrina and Baby doll.

While that chaos erupted downstairs Maddox and I opened the door to go meet Ice and are met with three goons. "Where you bitches going?" One asked as they grabbed me and Maddox. One pointed a gun at us "Stay cool and yall be alright." He snarls and waves the gun towards the elevator. I want to faint but mirror Maddox's energy and remain calm. In the elevator Maddox speaks up "You boys know were just workers right? Ya'll don't want us" she lightly giggles. "Bitch shut up." The one with the gun replies watching the defending numbers on the elevator display. "I can pay yall a million dollars a piece if yall let us go." Maddox offers. They all think for a minuet. "Ok ill make you a deal. Let me just deliver yall downstairs. If he wants to kill yall then ill save your life for a million dollars." The gunman replies. He must not be too bright because why would his plan make sense. He could of just said no one was up there instead of risking his life later.

"Thats not gonna work handsome. I can transfer you 3 million right now and you let us go when these doors open. Let me go in my backpack, my computer is right here" Maddox pleads. He shakes the gun in her direction. "Ahh you must think I'm dumb. If you just a worker how you got 3 million to send?" He asks like he just cracked the code to some prize. "Baby our team makes money. I'm going to send you all I have saved up." Maddox tries to convince the goons. "Nah bitch I already made my deal. Take it or shut up." He snarls. Maddox did good but this time she couldn't negotiate her way out.

When the elevators opened it was straight mayhem. Goons were fighting security and Biggs was on the ground taking the beating of his life. Sabrina and Baby doll were being restrained and watched helplessly. Maddox tapped my finger and pointed towards the front entrance with her eyes. She then tapped her chest and mouthed follow my lead. In two seconds Maddox yelled out "Biggs! Noooooooo!" Like she was so appalled by what was happening. She ran in his direction and I took off right behind her. The goons had a delayed reaction but took chase shortly there after. Maddox made a quick right and headed for the front door with me tight on her heels. J black looked up, noticed Maddox and yelled "Get that bitch!" Pointing in our direction. "Stay with them." He ordered his goons with the girls as he and the rest of his crew chased us to the door of the casino.

We dashed through slot machines zig zagging around customers and cocktail waitresses. J black stayed in hot pursuit flipping over trays and pushing people out of the way. Biggs at this time gained enough strength, got up off the floor and ran for the exit. The goons didn't know whether to chase him or let the girls go. They dragged Sabrina and babydoll towards the exit as fast as they could following behind everyone. Maddox and I ran out of the front door with J black and his good right behind us. “Freeze!” A cop yelled as dozens of them surrounded us with pistols drawn. Helicopters flew in the sky with the spotlight pointed at the entrance. Lights from police cars and cruisers lit up the parking lot like an amusement park. The cars and taxi’s that sit in front of the hotel began quickly pulling off trying to get out of the way as patrons screamed and began running. In the madness I lost sight of Maddox as the police surrounded the gang. Biggs exits unknowingly walking into the trap with the goons not far behind.

A few officers rush inside and arrest them all as they made their way to the exit. Outside they cuffed J black, and his goons as a female officer placed handcuffs on my wrist. Brian walks up in the middle of the commotion with his badge swinging around his neck. There goes those butterflies I got when I was around him. This time I realized it was a sign an enemy is around. He had a coldness about him as he approached. Out the side of my eye I see Ice driving slow on the other side of the entrance watching whats going on. I notion go with my head, winked and blew him a kiss. Brian noticed what I did and turned around to see who I was winking at. He was too late, Ice had pulled off.

He turned back to me, smiled and walked away. “Biggs I been looking for you my guy. You have the right to remain silent anything you say can and will be held against you....” Brian finished as he scanned the crowd. “Where’s Maddox?” He asked no one in particular. “This is everyone who was downstairs sir.” A young officer responds. “Then go check the room! Go look at the tapes! Find her!” Brian yells furiously.

A couple of officers run inside and head to the room and security desk. I smiled to myself as Brian turned his sights to me. “Where is she?” He snarls closely to my face. “She was right next to me when we came outside. I have no idea where she went. I would be with her.” I reply. “Kinda fucked up she left you.” He sarcastically implies and walks away.

Brian goes to review the tapes and see's Maddox hop into a cab as soon as the police run towards them with their guns drawn. The commotion of the patrons running inall directions caused a brief distraction. Maddox turns in my direction like she expected me to run with her but had no time to grab me. The taxi pulled off before the cops got close enough to arrest her. "Find this cab!" Brian charges as the officers scramble to find the cab company. Within 20 minuets they find the driver who reveals he dropped her off at the airport. The police officers take us to the precent as Brian and a few of his FBI buddies make a bee line for the airport. The drive over Brian puts out an APB on Maddox and sends her picture to airport security to prevent her from flying out. It was already too late Maddox was in the wind. The problem Brian had was he didn't know which name she would be flying under. He could send out her picture but an outfit change and wig can kill that instantly. He was furious.

After 3 hours they bought me out of the holding cell and into an interrogation room. Brian sat on the other end of the table with a thick folder skimming its contents. I sat down across from him wearing handcuffs the kind officers provided while transferring me. "Hey A'maya." Brian utters without looking up from his folder. I stared coldly at him waiting for him to get eye contact with me. "You maybe in a little trouble..." Brian reveals after Tati's arrest they followed her 24 hours a day. They saw our locations and the office that was set up. They did some digging on what we were up too and saw the building being bought in fictitious names. They investigated Charles and the commissioner. They have already warrants out and are going to be arrested for fraud. Apparently Biggs baby mother began cooperating months ago when they left LA. Thats why it was so hard for him to reach them. Brian asked Tati's and Maddox location.

He wore shame and embarrassment on his face. "They watching us from the other side of the window?" I question coldly. Brian nods. "Ok well you and I made a deal. Keep my mouth shut and I'm safe. I never said a word and I thought the company was legit. I got paid like a real job I had no other reason to think otherwise." Brian began to blush as I continued "So tell your friends about our deal or I can." I say with my face twisted up. He tried to stand his ground and ask about where Maddox was. He didn't threaten me with any jail time so I knew he had every intention on letting me go and this was all just to get information. I played into it. "Again Officer Brian. You know from our discussions from when you was under covers" I slip up purposely "that I have nothing to do with what she has going on. You even notice how she left me high and dry at the hotel." "She wanted you to go with her." He replies. "Huh" I say confused. Brian explains what he saw on the video tape and had I paid attention I probably would have been with her right now. That bought comfort to my heart because I was hurt thinking she abandoned me. "I don't know about any of that Officer Brian" I say again to annoy him. He asks me all type of questions about the organization. I never implement Tati, Maddox, Sabrina or Baby doll. He already told me they had a hard on for Biggs so I tell him what he wants to hear. Biggs is the brains and the rest of us are his minions. "Where's you little boyfriend?" Brian sarcastically snarls. "In front of me, I hope." I squint and blow him a kiss. "That'll be all. Bring in Lewis." Brians yells over my shoulder. He doesn't give me any eye contact.

I learn that Biggs tells on J black for his role in the scam and what they did to Pepsi. He blames them saying he was fearful for his life and under duress. They threatened him. They knew about his crimes for two years now they just couldn't catch him. Biggs was responsible for 3 murders back in Ohio and that's why he really left. Biggs was on the run from the police and the family of the victims. I wondered if Ice knew about this or was apart of it. Biggs blamed Maddox and said she was the mastermind. The cops lied and said Baby doll and Sabrina were cooperating so he threw them under the bus as well. For some reason I never heard him saying anything about me and Ice.

Sabrina and Baby doll took plea deals in exchange for testifying against Biggs and J black. I spent three days in that godforsaken jail before I released. Brian was outside when I walked out of the precent. "I kept my word A'maya." He announces a few feetaway. "Let me take you to the airport." He offers and opens the passenger side door to a police Suv. Inside was a shotgun tucked behind the seat facing upwards and a computer screen between the two seats near the dashboard. The backseat was gated and looked terribly uncomfortable on purpose. Brian hopped in and swerved into traffic effortlessly. He apologized for how things went and how he wasn't supposed to get close to me let alone fall for me. Brian claims to have been stuck in between his job and his feelings. He confessed falling hard for me and hates how everything turned out. I never meant for me to feel used and he regrets how everything turned out. I played nice until we got to the airport entrance. "Brian you truly are a piece of shit. You can get redemption somewhere else. You used me. So take your feelings and stick them up your goofy ass!" I yelled before slamming the door. I didn't have any luggage so that made my exit an easy one.
Brian just sat there and watched me walk out of his life until he lost sight of me.

The flight home was bitter sweet. I had my freedom, almost two million dollars, I'm going home but I am going alone. Maddox got away like she said she always would so that bought me comfort. Tati messaged me when Maddox didn't respond letting me know she's good. I informed her of what happened and told her to be safe. I encouraged her to go to school and do the right thing. She wasn't that much younger but I knew this kid was going to be alone for a minuet. I decided to build a relationship with her from that point on. My heart ached the entire flight for Ice. I couldn't contact him in fear of Brian still looking for him. I had to get a new phone when I landed and put it in my mother's name. I learned that much from Maddox. I hoped Maliak was good and I mourned Pepsi.

Biggs copped to life in prison instead of going to trail and face the death penalty. Sabrina and Baby doll got 5 years apart but the judge later suspended the sentence. Sabrina went back home to fight and get her mother out of jail. She figured she had enough money now for a good lawyer. Her grandparents were so happy to see her and her family welcomed her in. Baby doll left California and was never heard from again. As for the commissioner and Charles they both got arrested for fraud. Ice hadn't let go of what Charles did to me. He waited until he was in general population and had some Filipino gang members sodomize and beat him up pretty badly. Charles was hospitalized and his trail was delayed. Ice made sure whatever Charles was in jail he wasn't safe.

CHAPTER 25

"5,4,3,2,1...HAPPY NEW YEAR!! The crowd erupted as we all celebrated 2019 at the grand opening of my lounge on Lafayette street in Brooklyn! "Congratulations A'maya! I'm so proud of you!" My mother yelled over the music. I can't remember the last time she said that. Not even when I graduating community college. The venue was packed wall to wall with friends, family and fans. I had the crowd rocking with old school hiphop and r&b as we danced the night away. I really wished Maddox could be here I miss her so much it hurts. It has been almost two years since I have seen or spoken to her. I'm glad we set up a "what if" strategy and she followed my advice. Maddox left 1 million dollars in cash at her grandmothers vacation home in a childhood toy chest tucked away in the attic. She gave me a key and full access to invest for the partnership endeavors. The money was easy to clean because of my new cash business. The trust between us was strong but grew tremendously after that whole crazy ordeal. She would have loved the location and our 1st turn out but especially the name!

I hired an amazing chef straight out of culinary school who created an delicious menu of finger foods and a mixologist that created specialized drinks. Amari was dressed to the nines with a nurse he started dating 2 months ago. They locked lips and danced the night away. Tati flew into town to celebrate the opening of "Maddox" . It was so good to see her and she was doing exceptionally well. Tati went to nursing school and opened a recovery home for surgery patients while she was getting her degree. By the time she graduated she already had three of them set up in the Miami area. I was so proud of her.

We grabbed a table and caught up. James finally went back to school for cyber security and started his own firm. He invested his money and also has a few rental properties. I was so excited to hear about his success. "So why are you here?" I asked like an idiot. Just them Amari walk up and I introduce them. Amari reminds me that whoever really wanted me would come and get me. He bought James a shot and they clicked. "So back to you. I told you we were going to be together I just needed to be the man you deserved." He went on about once I left life didn't feel the same. Biggs wasn't there to manipulate him anymore. He felt alone even surrounded by so many women. He was at the doctor's office for a check up and ran into an old buddy who turned his life around. He encouraged James to get on the right path because the streets do not love anyone. That conversation really affected him. He revealed Malinda and Maliak doubled crossed him, robbed him of whatever they could take and disappeared. He later found out they fell in love and wanted to leave town as soon as we all got arrested. They swore Ice went down with us as well. I listened like it was only the two of us left on earth. God how did he get more handsome!? I felt bad for what happened to him but I was getting turned on with each passing second we sat here.

Unable to control myself I lean in and kiss him like I'm trying to catch up on all the affection I've been deprived all of this time. As he starts kissing me more intensely I stop him and lead the way to my office. James turned into an octopus as soon as the door closed, breathing heavy with his hands all over me. I moaned at each kiss passionately placed all over my face and neck. James ran his hands up my hips as his fingers found their way under my shirt.

It was 2:30 something in the morning , with party on tilt ,when he walked.
My heart almost leapt out of my chest at the sight of him.
He wore a fitted white button down shirt that hugged his muscular body.
He must have been working out cause damn he looks incredible.
His black slacks finished with black dress shoes matched his tie.
I never thought I'd see the day he would cut his hair,
but here he was with a low fade scanning the room for me.

I thought I hated this man. I leapt from the DJ booth and
ran to wrap my arms around him. My body melted against
his as I kissed those lips I missed so much.
He pulled me close and embraced me even more.
"I have missed you so A'maya" he mouths under the loud
music as he hands me a dozen bright red roses.
"I have missed you so so much Jay."

We all had to cut contact when shit hit the fan.
The feds use one phone tap to start looking at someone else.
So while they may focus on one target they investigate
anyone that person communicates with.
That car accident was Gods way of protecting
Ice or his guardian angel leading his path.
Makes sense now why Maliak wasn't injured.
"Who told you about the party?" I asked him with the bouquet to my nose.
"Social media!" He exclaimed.

His smooth hands were heated gloves exploring anywhere he could reach. The tequila misplaced my inhibitions making it hard to locate any of them. I do not remember how I ended up with my face pinned against the wall and James behind me driving himself inside of me. I exhaled with her thrust. The loud music drowned the moans from the both of us. James had one hand on the wall and the other hand around my neck from behind as he bit on my neck and ears. I missed his scent, I missed his touch, I missed HIM.

Ice and I finally rejoined the party which was clearly pushing 4 a.m. I walked Ice over and introduced him to my mother sitting with my aunts and a few of her friends. "Mommy this is James." I shyly announce. "Oh Mija he is handsome." She announces surrounded by grinning faces from the other women. He leans in to give my mom a hug and kiss on the hand. "Oh he's a keeper. Honey if she doesn't want you I'll take you!" My drunk aunt blurts out as the ladies join her in laughter. The night was electric and the sight of Ice felt like my life was complete. My mother always quoted the scripture "Whatever the devil meant for evil God will make good." Maybe all of tha madness was for Ice to get out of that dangerous lifestyle. I find the man of my dreams and get to open the lounge of my dreams. This is what happiness felt like. I am no way proud of how I obtained some of the money I have but looking back I do not regret a thing. I could only image how my future with James is going to be and how our children will look. I feel my phone buzzing in my back pocket. It is a message on WhatsApp from an international number I have never seen before. The letters HNY with a black, white, red and green flag. I googled it and it was for Abu Dhabi. I smiled knowing Maddox was safe. I text back ILY. She responds ILY2.

(Happy new year and I love you for those not too abbreviation savvy.)

THE END......For now

www.ingramcontent.com/pod-product-compliance
Lightning Source LLC
LaVergne TN
LVHW090559110826
845146LV00001B/188

* 9 7 9 8 9 9 4 2 0 4 0 1 6 *